"Did you have another date lined up tonight?"

"This isn't a date. It's a business meeting."

"Do you kiss all of your business associates, or just me?"

Stumped, unable to think of a fitting response, Grace slanted her head to the left and hitched a hand to her hips. The next time Jackson said something smart to her, or flashed that stupid "I'm the man" grin, it was on. She'd had enough of his fresh mouth for one night.

"It's your fault we're even in this stupid mess," she grumbled.

"How was I supposed to know the door was locked? It's never locked."

"This wouldn't have happened if you weren't showing off."

Jackson pointed a finger at his chest. "You're blaming me for trying to impress you?" he asked, shock evident in his voice. "Have you looked in the mirror lately?"

Grace pretended his words didn't faze her, but inwardly her heart was dancing.

"You're stunning, and captivating in every sense of the word, and I'll do anything to make you smile, including showing off my one-of-a-kind specialty cakes."

Dear Reader,

Have you ever felt an immediate connection to someone? Mind-blowing chemistry you couldn't deny or control? That's what happens to Jackson Drayson when he meets Grace Nichols. His plan? To win her heart. But things go awry during their first date. He burns dinner, then accidently locks them in the bakery freezer. Though all isn't lost. Jackson has seduction on his mind, and will stop at nothing to prove he's the only man she needs.

Grace is torn. Should she remain loyal to her family or follow her heart? It's an impossible decision to make, and secretly dating Jackson—her father's sworn enemy—only complicates matters. The dreamy baker is sweet and romantic, charming, too, and his kisses are as scrumptious as his pastries. Grace and Jackson are a perfect match, and I think you'll agree.

I enjoyed writing this series with my Kimani sisters, Yahrah St. John (*Cappuccino Kisses*), and Jamie Pope (*Love and a Latte*), and I'm eagerly looking forward to our next one! :-)

All the best in life and love,

Pamela Yaye

Mocha Pleasures

PAMELA YAYE

HARLEQUIN® KIMANI™ ROMANCE

Recycling programs
for this product may
not exist in your area.

ISBN-13: 978-0-373-86462-1

Mocha Pleasures

HARLEQUIN®

Printed in U.S.A.

™ www.Harlequin.com

Pamela Yaye has a bachelor's degree in Christian education. Her love for African-American fiction prompted her to pursue a career in writing romance. When she's not working on her latest novel, this busy wife, mother and teacher is watching basketball, cooking or planning her next vacation. Pamela lives in Alberta, Canada, with her gorgeous husband and adorable, but mischievous, son and daughter.

Books by Pamela Yaye

Harlequin Kimani Romance

Visit the Author Profile page at Harlequin.com for more titles.

Acknowledgments

I want to thank my husband, Jean-Claude,
for his love, support and guidance. I couldn't have
written twenty-three Harlequin Kimani Romance
novels without you, Papito, and I appreciate everything
you do for me and the kids. You mean the world to me,
and I'm grateful to have you in my life.
Thank you for allowing me to live my dream.

Chapter 1

Jackson "Jack" Drayson stood behind the counter of his family's bakery, Lillian's of Seattle, spotted the mother of two struggling to get her deluxe stroller inside the crowded, bustling shop and felt a rush of compassion. Reaching the family in three strides, he pulled open the front door and stepped aside to let them enter. "Welcome to Lillian's of Seattle."

"Thank you so much," the mother said, her tone filled with gratitude.

"It's my pleasure." Jackson wore a boyish smile. "I've always had a thing for redheads with freckles."

Her eyes brightened, and she giggled like a kid at the circus. "You do?"

"Yes, so if you need anything just ask. I love helping beautiful women."

Another high-pitched laugh. "You just made my day!"

Jackson knew the compliment had guaranteed the

bakery a sale. It always did. At twenty-eight, he'd per-
fected the art of flirting, and knew Chase would be
proud of him for charming another customer. A savvy
accountant with a thirst for success, his thirty-one-
year-old brother was the perfect person to oversee the
financial operations at the bakery. To ensure the bakery's success, Chase had taken a leave of absence from
his high-powered corporate job, and when he wasn't
wooing his fiancée—talented jewelry designer Amber
Bernard—he was working hard to boost sales. Chase
and Amber were on a pre-honeymoon trip at a luxury
hotel overlooking Snoqualmie Falls. Jackson hadn't
heard from his brother since he'd left town yesterday
and didn't expect to. Chase was with Amber, and when
his lady love was around, nothing else mattered to his
big brother.

Glancing around the bakery, Jackson remembered
the first time Chase approached him about an exciting
new business venture.

They were at Samson's Gym, talking smack, lifting
weights and eyeing the ladies. Chase suggested going
to work for the Draysons, and Jackson had laughed out
loud. Hell, no. He'd always resented the Chicago branch
of the family. Why were they so high and mighty? Why
had they shut out their Seattle relatives for so long?
More persuasive than a politician, Chase had convinced
him that a bakery would be an excellent business opportunity, and posed it as a challenge. What if they
could make Lillian's of Seattle more profitable than
the Chicago store? What if they became the number-
one bakery in town? Jack had never been able to walk
away from a challenge or a dare, and when Chase suggested he was afraid they weren't good enough to "keep

up with the Draysons," Jack was in. Though, initially, he didn't think he could work with his perfectionist brother. Where Chase had always been a methodical rule-follower, Jackson's favorite motto was By Any Means Necessary. He often wondered if he could have been adopted, because he was so different from his siblings. He'd attended three different colleges, and had quickly gotten bored by the classes, the course work and the dreary study groups. His faculty mentor told him he was smart, with a great mind for business, but his dislike of convention had often gotten in his way. He'd finally graduated from Seattle University with a business degree but he could have just as easily obtained a degree in science, math or history.

"Wow, I heard this place was nice, but that's an understatement." Wearing an awestruck expression on her chubby face, the mother of two slowly took in her surroundings. "It looks more like a high-end boutique than a bakery."

Her words filled Jackson with pride. Everything about the shop reeked of class and sophistication—the large gold script bearing Lillian's name on the front door, the gold chandeliers, the glass cases holding bite-sized pastries, and the attractive tables and chairs inside the adjoining café, Myers Coffee Roasters. Located in Denny Triangle, a residential and professional community teeming with restaurants, bars, specialty shops and parks, the bakery had opened to rave reviews two months earlier and was now a Seattle favorite.

"I don't know what to order. Everything looks amazing."

"That's because it is," Jackson said confidently. "At Lillian's of Seattle, we believe in using only natural ingredients, so whether you choose a double-fudge brownie or a slice of pecan pie, you can be sure that it's one hundred percent fresh and one hundred percent delicious. Our mission is to make Seattle happier and tastier, and we will. One decadent dessert at a time."

Thanking him again, the mother wandered off in search of a sweet treat.

Customers streamed through the open door and Jackson greeted everyone with a nod and a smile. The aromas of baked apples, cinnamon and freshly brewed coffee wafted out of the kitchen, reminding Jackson of all the summers he'd visited his great-aunt Lillian in Chicago and worked at her bakery. There he'd gained a love of cooking and developed a keen interest in the family business. His parents, Graham and Nadia, thought he was wasting his time at Lillian's. A savvy real estate agent and self-made man, his father had built a successful life for himself in Seattle and wanted the same for his children. Last week at Sunday dinner his mother had admonished him to quit baking and find a "real" job. A *man's* job. Jackson didn't let her comments get to him. Instead he let them roll off his back. He wasn't going to bail on Chase and Mariah—or disappoint his great-aunt—and he wanted to make Lillian's a success.

The mood inside the bakery was festive and Jackson noted customers were talking, laughing and stuffing their faces with pastries. Thanks to his twenty-six-year-old sister, Mariah, the bakery had quickly become a popular hangout spot for stay-at-home moms, chic twenty-somethings and college students. A former advertising assistant at a billion-dollar food company, she put her knowledge and training to good use. She ensured everything ran smoothly at Lillian's and had proved to be a skilled baker, as well. Everyone had an important role at the bakery. Chase was the brains, Mariah was the talent and Jackson not only made specialty cakes, but he was also the face of the company, the unofficial spokesperson. He loved people—especially women—and since most of their customers were females, he manned the register, chatted them up and encouraged them to return. They always did. Chase believed Jackson was Lillian's secret weapon and Jackson appreciated his brother's faith in him.

Jackson checked the time on his platinum wristwatch. Where was Mariah? She used to be the first one at the bakery, but these days she spent more time with her millionaire boyfriend, Everett Myers, than she did at the shop. Jackson teased her for falling head-over-heels for the widowed coffee importer and his eight-year-old son, EJ, but he was secretly thrilled for her. Chase, too. His siblings had found love, and even though Jackson had zero desire to settle down or have a family of his own, he was happy for them. Love would never be in the cards for him. He easily got bored, craved spontaneity and excitement, and couldn't imagine wanting to be with the same person for the rest of his life.

"Good morning," a blonde cooed, sailing through the open door.

"Welcome to Lillian's," he greeted. "If you need anything just let me know."

"I will." Winking lasciviously, she licked her lips. "You can bet on it."

Glancing outside, Jackson was surprised to see the weather had changed from a warm and sunny June morning to windy and overcast. He'd been too busy baking to notice. He had to make a baseball-themed cake for a fiftieth birthday party, and since he didn't want to disappoint the owner of the Seattle Mariners, he'd started working on it bright and early that morning.

A wistful smile found his lips. Two months at Lillian's and it still blew Jackson's mind that he was a baker. After watching seven seasons of *Cake Boss*, and several online tutorials, he'd tried his hand at making a three-tier fondant cake for Chase and Amber's engagement party. Not only did Mariah love the elaborate design, she'd also said it tasted delicious and commissioned him to make samples for the bakery. Within a week, he had so many orders to fill he'd had to hire another baker to keep up with the demand. His specialty cakes were a hit, and Jackson was confident his one-of-a-kind chocolate creation would wow guests at the party on Friday night.

"Good morning. Welcome to…"

His eyes fell across the tall, willowy woman standing outside at the crosswalk at Denny Way, and Jackson lost his train of thought. Couldn't speak. Feeling his knees buckle, he leaned against the door to support his weight. Everything screeched to a halt as he gazed at the attractive female in the sleeveless blue dress. Her pixie cut drew attention to her big doe eyes, her lush pink lips and blinding white teeth. There was something sad and pensive about her, a vulnerability he found oddly appealing. She wore a don't-mess-with-me expression on her face and her arms were crossed, but there was no disputing her beauty.

Jackson openly admired her, told himself to quit staring but he couldn't look away. She was a stunner. Beautiful cleavage, slim hips, curves that made his mouth water. He was a leg man, had been since the first time he'd seen Tyra Banks on the cover of *Black Men* magazine back in the day, and the woman had a long, sleek pair. *The model doesn't have a damn thing on her*, he thought, his gaze gliding down her thighs, his hands itching to follow suit.

Intrigued, he continued watching her. The older gentleman standing to her left in the charcoal-grey suit tapped her on the shoulder, but Luscious Lips was having none of it. Giving him her back, she stared intently at the traffic light and the moment it changed she left the stranger in her dust. She moved with poise, carried herself with inherent grace, and Jackson knew she came from money. His gaze zeroed in on her left hand. No ring. That meant she was fair game. Women who looked like her—young, supple and hot—always had several boyfriends, and if by some stroke of good luck she was single, it was by choice.

Jackson was so busy staring at her, admiring her sexy, mesmerizing strut and every swish of her hips, he didn't realize she'd breezed into the bakery until the scent of her perfume tickled his nostrils.

Snapping to attention, he straightened to his full height and checked his black T-shirt and khaki pants for any traces of flour. Like everyone in the room, he immediately took notice of her. Drawn to her, he trailed her around the store at a distance as she moved from one display to the next, carefully perusing the baked goods inside. Her big brown eyes missed nothing, read the handwritten note cards above each case as if she was about to be quizzed on the content. Minutes passed, but Luscious Lips still didn't place an order.

Catching himself gawking at her, Jackson warned

himself to get a grip. Luscious Lips marched toward the register and he slid behind the counter, curious about the woman with the model good-looks. She smelled of peaches and jasmine, an intoxicating scent that wreaked havoc on his body. He couldn't get his thoughts in order, couldn't get his mouth to work, and felt an erection stab the zipper of his jeans. Heat singed his cheeks, drenching his skin with perspiration. Jackson couldn't think of anything but kissing her, ravishing her with his mouth. He was dying to touch her, wanted to caress her from her shoulders to her hips, and between her thighs.

"Are you going to help me, or stand there staring off into space?"

Her tone was clipped, full of annoyance, but she had a lovely voice. The gap between her two front teeth enhanced her one-of-a-kind look. The more Jackson stared at her the more he wanted her, desired her, imagined himself stealing a kiss from her plump, moist lips. "I'm Jackson Drayson, one of the owners of this fine establishment."

Her eyebrows drew together in a questioning slant, but she didn't speak.

"Lillian's is Seattle's favorite bakery, and I'm confident you'll love our pastries, especially our baguettes and croissants. They're better than the ones they make in France!"

"You're not the only bakery in town."

"That's true," he conceded, "but I've tried the others and they're not even in our league. Our baked goods are the best in town, and we'll prove it next month at Bite of Seattle."

A scowl bruised her delicate features. "For a newcomer, you're awfully sure of yourself."

"Draysons always are, and for good reason. Our sister company, Lillian's of Chicago, has been in business for over forty years, but its humble beginnings won't stop us from expanding our beloved pastry empire and winning the hearts of Americans."

"Thanks for the history lesson."

To let her know he was interested, he wore a broad grin and leaned over the counter. "What's your name, beautiful, and when can I take you out? Is tomorrow soon enough?"

"I don't mean to be rude, but I came here to eat, not to make a love connection."

An awkward silence fell between them, but Jackson wanted to make her smile. Down but not out, he spoke in a casual, relaxed tone, refusing to show that her words had rattled his confidence. "You must be a foodie," he joked, determined to brighten her mood, "because I've never seen anyone take twenty minutes to decide what to order."

"Is that a crime?" she quipped. "I didn't realize I was being timed."

His gaze strayed from her eyes to her lips. He liked watching them move, imagined how they'd feel around his— Jackson slammed the brakes on the explicit thought. Luscious Lips was stunning, no doubt, one of the sexiest women he'd ever seen in the flesh, but he could do without her brusque tone and frosty attitude.

"I'll have a pistachio cupcake."

Jackson punched in her order, and took the ten-dollar bill from her outstretched hand. Their fingers touched, brushed against each other, causing an electric current to shoot through his body. He stood, frozen in place, his leather Kenneth Cole shoes rooted to the floor, unable to move. Their attraction, the chemistry crackling between them, was so potent it consumed the air, made it impossible for Jackson to do anything but stare at her. Embarrassed by his physical response to her touch, he broke the spell by giving his head a shake and expelling a deep breath. He had to get ahold of himself, or he'd be the laughingstock of the bakery. His employees were watching him, all wearing the same puzzled expressions on their faces, and Jackson wanted to kick himself for acting like a horny teen.

Man, snap out of it! yelled his inner voice. *You're a player, not a scrub, so get your head in the game, or she'll never, ever give you the time of day.*

"Can I get my change? I'm pressed for time, and I don't want to be late for work."

Snapping out of his thoughts, he nodded, and gave Luscious Lips her money. Seconds later, he handed over her purchase. He expected her to turn and march off—giving him another view of her perfectly round backside—but she opened the dainty white take-out box, immediately took out the cupcake and tasted it. Surprise flashed in her eyes, and Jackson didn't know if that was good or bad. Once again, he was captivated, unable to look away.

She chewed slowly, thoughtfully, and then said to herself, "The vanilla extract is excessive. Half a teaspoon would have been more than enough."

Jackson raised an eyebrow. *What? Where does she get off criticizing my baking?* He'd followed the recipe to a T and customers had been raving about his cupcakes all morning. Oddly enough, he was insulted by her critique *and* turned on. Luscious Lips obviously knew something about baking, and how to leave a man breathless. As she marched out the door, swishing her shapely hips, Jackson felt his pulse throb in his ears.

Curious, he opened the case, grabbed a pistachio cupcake from the top shelf and took a bite. The cupcake was moist and flavorful, but the vanilla extract *was* excessive. Dang it if she wasn't right! His desire for Luscious Lips cooled, evaporating like smoke. Jackson loved women, and in all his twenty-eight years he'd never met a female he didn't like—until now. Why did she have to be so cold? Why did she have to dog his baking? Didn't she know how hard it was to wake up at 5:00 a.m. and bake hundreds of pastries after a night of clubbing?

Hearing his cell phone buzz, he took it out of his back pocket and punched in his password. He had two new text messages. As usual, Diego was checking up on him. He'd call his buddy during his lunch break to touch base with him. Jackson considered Diego Maldonado—his friend since the fifth grade—and his large, loving, Portuguese brood to be his second family. Reading the second text, he couldn't believe his good luck. His ex-girlfriend wanted to know if he was free tomorrow night. She had two front-row tickets for the T.I. concert, and VIP passes for the after party at Trinity Nightclub. Did he want to go?

Hell, yeah, Jackson thought, immediately responding to her message. He'd dated the paralegal for three months, but called it quits when she started dropping not-so-subtle hints about moving into his Beacon Hill bachelor pad. They weren't soul mates, but they'd always be great friends. Jackson hung out with all of his exes—except Mimi. They hadn't spoken since he'd called off their engagement last year, and he had no in-tention of ever speaking to Mimi Tanaka again. As far as Jackson was concerned, she was dead to him.

Remembering the night they broke up, he realized he'd dodged a bullet by ending their relationship. Marriage wasn't for everyone, and Jackson was smart enough to realize it wasn't for him. He had decades of bachelorhood ahead of him, years of skirt chasing to enjoy, and he wasn't going to screw that up by getting hitched. His brother and sister were over-the-moon in love, walking around the bakery all day long with permanent smiles on their faces, but Jackson had zero desire to find love. That didn't mean he didn't value and respect women. He did. Thought they were exciting, fascinating creatures, and for that reason just one would never do.

"We're running low on éclairs and we're out of lemon scones, as well…"

Jackson blinked, returning to the present. Kelsey Andrews, an intern from the Seattle Culinary Academy, sidled up beside him, eyes bright, smile in place, curls tumbling around her face. Yesterday after work she'd invited him to Zani Bar for drinks, but he'd turned her down, lied and said he had plans with his dad. Kelsey was ten years his junior, and he didn't want to give her the wrong idea or encourage her advances. Workplace romances never worked, and if he hooked up with the fresh-faced barista, Mariah would kick his ass.

"If you don't mind manning the till, I'll head to the kitchen and make another batch."

"No problem," she purred, her gaze full of longing. "Anything for you, Jackson."

Put off by her seductive tone, Jackson stalked out of the bakery and into the bright, spacious kitchen. He grabbed an oversized mixing bowl and the ingredients he needed from the cupboard. Getting down to work, he put all thoughts of Luscious Lips out of his mind. She wasn't the only beautiful woman in town, and if she didn't want to go out with him it was her loss, not his. He had things to do, had to finish the pastries before the insane lunch rush, but this time when he made pistachio cupcakes he'd go easy on the vanilla extract.

Despite himself, he wore a rueful smile. What a morning. *What a woman*, he thought, remembering their terse exchange. Jackson was mad at himself for not getting her name. He wished he knew more about her besides her penchant for pistachio cupcakes. He had a feeling Luscious Lips would return to Lillian's one day soon, felt it in his gut, and when she did he was going to get her name *and* her phone number—even if it meant using every trick in his arsenal.

Chapter 2

"You did what?" Doug Nicholas roared.

He cursed, yelling so loud it caused the window inside his elegantly decorated office at Sweetness Bakery to shake. The room was filled with vibrant area rugs, cozy chairs and potted plants, but Grace would rather be at the dentist than stuck in her father's office, listening to him rant and rave about how irresponsible she was. She was a twenty-six-year-old woman with a strong head on her shoulders, but he made her feel like a screwup.

"What were you thinking? Have you lost your mind?"

Of average height, with thinning grey hair and eyeglasses perched on his nose, he had a grumpy disposition and spoke in a low, clipped tone. He was rough around the edges, gruff at times, but Grace loved him with all her heart. "Dad, calm down—"

"What possessed you to go to Lillian's?" he said, speaking through clenched teeth. "What if a reporter was on hand and snapped a picture of you stuffing your face at our competitor's shop? Do you know how embarrassing that would be?"

Grace bit her tongue, didn't dare answer because it wasn't a rhetorical question, and she didn't want to make the situation worse. Swallowing a yawn, she snuck a glance at her wristwatch. It was eight o'clock and the bakery was closed for the day, but her father was making such a fuss she feared the cleaning crew would come running. Grace managed Sweetness, had since her mother's untimely death, but her father was always on hand to help. It had been a banner year for the bakery, but Doug wasn't satisfied, never was. They had an exceptional team that loved Sweetness Bakery, just as Rosemary had, and she knew her mother was smiling down on them. Thinking about her mom made her heart ache. Grace would do anything to see her again, to hug her, to hear her voice just one more time. "Dad, relax, it wasn't that serious."

"Don't tell me to relax," he snapped. "You could have humiliated the shop, and caused irreversible damage! Your behavior was dumb and reckless."

His words stung, bruised her feelings, but Grace straightened in her chair and projected confidence, not fear. She'd made the right decision. She'd had no choice but to march into the splashy new bakery after reading the food blogs during her commute to work. According to bloggers, Lillian's was the best thing to ever happen to Seattle. Their cupcakes were divine, the ambiance darling, the staff personable and attentive, the location a winner. Unfortunately, Grace had to agree. She couldn't deny the truth. Her visit had been memorable—and not just because she'd met the hunky owner, Jackson Drayson—and she was curious if all of their pastries were to-die-for, or just the pistachio cupcakes. "Dad, I was merely checking out the competition and I'm glad I did. Now that we know what we're up against we can formulate a plan."

A pensive expression on his face, he stroked his pointy jaw. "What did you find out?"

That the picture in the *Seattle Times* of Jackson Drayson at Lillian's grand opening in April didn't do the baker justice! Grace felt a nervous flutter inside her belly. *He's even sexier in person, and his voice is so seductive I shivered when he spoke to me. Add to that, his cologne, like his smile, was intoxicating.*

"Don't keep me in suspense," Doug admonished. "Spill it."

Grace chose her words carefully, didn't reveal everything at once. She told her dad about her visit that morning, but didn't mention her run-in with Jackson. It wasn't important. *He* wasn't important, and she didn't want to waste time talking about him. She'd sized him up in five seconds flat. He was a lady-killer, a man who took great pleasure in seducing women—not her type in the least. Jackson Drayson was the personification of the term *deadly sexy*, and when she'd entered the bakery she noticed every female in the room was staring at the dreamy baker with lust in her eyes. The man was an attention seeker who wasn't happy unless women were fawning all over him, and Grace planned to stay far away from Mr. Smug.

"Tell me more." Doug leaned forward in his leather

chair. "Was the bakery packed? What is the mood and feel of the shop? Did you enjoy the cupcake?"

Grace answered her dad's questions the best she could. The more she spoke the more stress lines wrinkled her father's forehead. She'd never seen him like this—fidgeting with his hands, shifting around on his chair, grumbling under his breath—and feared he was having a nervous breakdown.

"I owe you an apology. You were right. Checking out Lillian's was a smart move."

"Thanks, Dad, and now I think it's the perfect time to implement some of the changes we spoke about last month," she said, feeling a rush of excitement. "Seattle has the best indie artists in the country, and I think we should showcase their talents at Sweetness. We can extend our weekend hours and offer two-for-one specials, as well. Poetry Fridays and Talent Night Saturdays will definitely attract new customers."

"This is a bakery, Grace. Not *America's Got Talent*."

"Dad, at least consider it—"

"There's nothing to consider. It's a stupid idea and we're not doing it. Case closed."

Flinching, as if slapped across the face, she dropped her gaze to her lap and blinked back the tears in her eyes. It was moments like this Grace wished she had siblings. Someone else she could vent to about the bakery, her promotional ideas, her dreams of moving to New York. After graduating from the Seattle Culinary Academy, she'd planned to relocate to the Big Apple to take the culinary world by storm. But it wasn't to be. Her mother's death had changed everything. She'd put her plans on ice and devoted her time and energy to growing the family business. To better aid her dad, she'd enrolled in graduate school and acquired a master's degree in accounting and financial management. It was tough, working at the bakery during the day and attending school at night, but she'd pulled through and graduated at the top of her class.

Her gaze fell across the framed photographs hanging on the ivory walls. Images of her mother—cutting the ribbon at the bakery's opening in the early eighties, rolling cookie dough, laughing with customers, manning the till—brought a sad smile to her lips. Her dad could be stubborn and narrow-minded at times, but he was the only family she had left. Since she'd never do anything to disrespect him, she held her tongue.

"Now is not the time to shake things up. We could alienate customers." Grunting, he scooped up the papers on his desk and shook his hands in the air. "Lillian's of Seattle opened a couple months ago, but they're already cutting into our profits. Sales are down nine percent since April, and those jerks are the reason why. We have to stop them before it's too late."

"Dad, what are you saying?"

A devilish gleam darkened his face. Her father had a reputation for playing dirty, for outwitting his business rivals with skillful maneuvers, but Grace wanted no part of his schemes. It wasn't her. Wasn't in her DNA to be sneaky and underhanded, and she didn't want to do anything she'd live to regret. Her mother's words came back to her, playing in her ears loud and clear. *Be a woman of integrity*, she'd admonished one afternoon while they were baking pastries for a two-hundred-guest baby shower. *And don't let anyone change who you are.*

"Your mother built Sweetness through blood, sweat

and tears, and it's more than just a bakery. It's her legacy, and I'd never forgive myself if I lost this place."

"Dad, you won't. Sweetness has been the leading bakery in Seattle for decades and that will never change. Our customers are loyal and they won't desert us."

"I won't lose to a bunch of rich kids who've had everything in life handed to them, who've never had to work for anything. It's not going to happen because I won't let it."

Grace wanted to correct him, to tell her dad that based on what she'd read and seen about Jackson Drayson his assumption couldn't be further from the truth. But she knew it was a bad idea to defend the enemy. Her mind returned to their conversation that morning. She vividly remembered his scent, the sound of his voice, how his eyes twinkled with mischief when he'd asked her out. Reflecting on their exchange, Grace wished she hadn't been so mean to him. She heard the talk around the bakery, and in her upscale Bellevue neighborhood. She knew what men said about her. They called her the Ice Queen, a man hater, and complained she was more difficult than a pop star.

Painful memories flooded her heart, piercing her soul like a dagger. Before Phillip Davies, she'd always thought the best of people, but after their bitter breakup she'd lost faith in not only men, but also her ability to choose the right one. Love was overrated. For women who believed in fairy tales. A waste of time, and she'd vowed never to put herself out there again. Why bother? Love didn't last, didn't work, and Grace wanted no part of it.

Seeing Jackson's image in her mind's eye, despite

her futile attempts to block it out, Grace wondered if
he had a girlfriend. She snorted, snickering inwardly.
Of course he had a girlfriend. Probably several. One
for every day of the week, and in every state, no doubt.
Not that she cared. Everything about the overconfident
baker screamed *player*—his swagger, his bad-boy grin,
the tattoo on his left bicep that said "Live each day as
if it's your last." And since he wasn't her type, Grace
shook off her thoughts and stood. It had been another
ten-hour day and she was beat. She wanted nothing
more than to crawl into bed and fall asleep. "Dad, I'm
tired. If it's okay with you, I'll prepare the profit-and-
loss statements in the morning."

"On your way in tomorrow, stop in at Lillian's and
sample something else." Doug snapped his fingers. "I
know. Buy one of those dragnet things they're advertising all over the place. I want to see what all the fuss
is about. The food critic for the *Seattle Times* said 'It's
heaven in your mouth' but I think she's exaggerating.
You know how women are."

"Dad, I don't think returning to Lillian's is a good
idea."

His eyes dimmed, and a frown pinched his thin lips.
"Why not?"

*Because I'm attracted to Jackson Drayson's light
brown eyes, full lips shaped by a trimmed goatee and
muscled biceps. I'm liable to trip and fall flat on my
face the next time he smiles at me!*

Knowing she couldn't tell the truth, she said the first
thing that came to mind. "If I go back it might raise
suspicions."

"Nonsense. They have no idea who you are." Doug
waved off her concerns with a flick of his hands. "It's

crucial you find out more about Lillian's. If we're going to crush them—and we will—we need to gather more intel, so return to the bakery and uncover their secrets."

Her shoulders sagged and panic ballooned inside her chest. It was official. Her dad had lost it. Gone off the deep end. And now, more than ever, she missed her mom. Rosemary had died fourteen months ago and not a day went by that Grace didn't think about her. Losing her mom had been a devastating blow, and if not for her father she never would have survived Rosemary's death. He'd been her anchor, her rock, and although she couldn't shake the feeling that she was making a mistake, she asked, "Dad, what do you want me to do?"

For the first time since she'd entered his office an hour earlier, her dad's face brightened and he grinned like a five-year-old who'd been given a new bike. "Maybe you can fake food poisoning or a nasty spill as you leave the shop. Bad publicity will drive customers away from Lillian's and straight through our doors."

Too shocked to speak, Grace dropped back down in her chair, her mind reeling. Her dad mistook her silence as acquiescence and offered one nefarious idea after another. Grace struggled to make sense of what he was saying and couldn't believe this was the same man who'd raised her to be an honest, trustworthy person. He loved money, would do anything to make more, and hated that Lillian's was cutting into his profits. For that reason he was willing to break the rules. Speaking in an animated voice, he encouraged her to return to the bakery, admonished her to befriend the baristas, and even the owners.

"Grace, are you in?"

Feeling trapped, her lips too numb to move, she slowly nodded.

"That's my girl!"

Chuckling, he rose from his chair and came around the desk.

Standing on wobbly legs, Grace dug her sandals into the carpet to steady herself.

"We got so caught up talking about Lillian's, I forgot why I asked you to come to my office in the first place," he said, shaking his head as if annoyed with himself. "I'm having Mr. and Mrs. Ventura over for brunch next Sunday, and I want you there."

Grace thought hard, but couldn't recall ever meeting the couple. "Who?"

"Mr. Ventura is an anesthesiologist, his wife is a pharmacist, and they own a slew of pharmacies on the west coast. They're a wealthy, well-connected couple with friends in high places, and I'm dying to join their social circle. Hence, the dinner party."

"Dad, I can't. I have roller derby practice at noon. "

He snorted. "I wish you'd quit that stupid team."

"And I wish you wouldn't work 24/7."

"If I host a dinner party on the twentieth, will you come?"

Grace had a game that afternoon, but she didn't tell her dad. Didn't want to upset him. "Sure, Dad," she said with a forced smile. "I'll bring the wine."

"Wear something nice," he advised. "They're bringing their son and he's single."

"That's nice, but I'm not interested."

"You should be. Ainsworth Ventura owns a profitable management company and was recently named entrepreneur of the year. Do you know what dating him could do for us?"

Grace didn't know, didn't care and had zero desire to meet the Seattle businessman.

"Like you, he's ready to settle down and start a family."

"Settling down is the furthest thing from my mind—"

"You'll change your mind once you meet Ainsworth. He's a ridiculously wealthy young man with everything going for him. Google him. You'll see that I'm right."

Yawning, she reached into her pocket for her cell phone, curious if her girlfriend Bronwyn Johansson had answered the text she'd sent that morning. They hadn't seen each other in a week, and Grace was looking forward to catching up with her bestie.

"Think you can make some of your apple beignets and toffee cookie bars for dessert?"

Grace shifted her weight from one foot to the next, fidgeting with her fingers. She hadn't set foot in the kitchen since her mother's death and didn't plan to. She used to love baking, would spend hours experimenting in the kitchen, but without Rosemary at her side, cooking held no appeal. These days she worked in the back office, managing the bakery the best she could. "No. I can't," she said, unable to shake her melancholy feelings.

"The regulars keep asking when you'll be back in the kitchen and I want to know, too."

"I don't know. I just don't feel up to it right now."

"Grace, it's been fourteen months. You have to move on."

Her stomach churned and pain stabbed her heart. Was there a time limit on grief? A predetermined

mourning period her therapist had failed to mention to
her? Grace wanted to turn the tables on her dad, wanted
to ask him when *he* was going to quit hiding out in his
office and start living again, but knew better than to
question him. "Dad, I'm beat. I'm going home."

"All right. Good night, pumpkin. Text me when you
get home."

Living at home wasn't ideal, especially when Grace
wanted to entertain, but whenever she broached the subject of finding her own place, her dad got upset, said he
couldn't stand to live in the house alone, and she'd bury
the idea. He still missed her mom, continued to grieve
her death over a year later, and balked whenever Grace
encouraged him to join a social club, or try online dating. "Don't worry, Dad. I will. I always do."

"I know. You're such a good girl. The best daughter
a father could ever ask for."

He wasn't one to show affection; Grace was shocked
when her dad hugged her and kissed her cheek. She
couldn't remember the last time he'd held her, and she
was comforted by his touch. Hearing her cell phone,
she took it out of the pocket of her blazer and glanced
discreetly at the screen. Grace groaned inwardly. What
did Phillip want now? He was as annoying as a pesky
mosquito, buzzing around in the dead of night, and she
was sick of him blowing up her phone. Why was he calling her? Couldn't he take a hint? It was the third time
he'd phoned her that afternoon, but since Grace had
nothing to say to him she let the call go to voice mail.

"We need to work together to save your mother's
shop," her father said quietly, sorrow flickering across
his strong facial features. "I'm counting on you to come
through for me."

"Dad, I will. I'll do whatever it takes to keep Sweetness on top. I promise." But as the impassioned declaration left her mouth, Grace knew it was a lie.

Chapter 3

This is so *wrong. I shouldn't be here*, Grace thought,
her conscience plagued with guilt. *I should be at Sweetness getting caught up on paperwork, not sitting here
like a groupie hoping to catch a glimpse of Jackson
"player extraordinaire" Drayson.*

Seated at a corner table inside Myers Coffee Roasters
café, sipping an espresso topped with oodles of whipped
cream, Grace watched the comings and goings inside
Lillian's with keen interest, wondering where the man
of the hour was.

For the second time in minutes Grace glanced at her
watch, then around the room. She didn't see Jackson
anywhere and she'd been looking out for him since arriving at the bakery an hour earlier. Grace was filled
with mixed emotions. Relief, because she turned into
a jittery fool whenever Jackson was around, and dis-

appointment, because she enjoyed their playful banter. On Monday he'd teased her for ignoring him, on Wednesday he'd complimented her BCBG keyhole dress—claimed he couldn't keep his eyes off of her—then suggested *she* take *him* out for a romantic dinner. He'd slipped a handwritten note into her purse when she wasn't looking, and finding it hours later made her heart smile. It was a cute gesture, one that made her crack up every time she reread his message, but Grace couldn't call him, not without looking desperate, so she hid the note in her top drawer and deleted all thoughts of Jackson from her mind.

Ha! barked her inner voice. *If you were trying to forget him you wouldn't be in* his *bakery.*

Grace lowered her coffee mug from her lips and cranked her head to the right. Every time the door chimed her heart raced. *Where is he?* Did Jackson have the day off? Was he out with one of his girlfriends? Wining, dining and seducing his flavor of the week? Of course he was, Grace decided. The baker was an affable, laid-back guy who obviously loved women, and it would be wise to keep her distance.

Reflecting on their heated exchange the day they'd met, Grace wished she hadn't let Jackson get under her skin. It was clear from then on that she was going to have her hands full with the hottie baker, and yesterday he'd been in fine form. Every time she entered Lillian's he was charming his female customers, and when Grace pointed it out to him, he'd teased her for being jealous and insisted she wanted him all to herself.

Snorting in disgust, she shook her head at the memory. Grace couldn't believe his nerve, how smug he was. To keep her anger in check she'd had to bite her tongue. Despite her misgivings about her "assignment" she'd stopped in at Lillian's every day to sample something new. Peanut-butter-sandwich cookies on Monday, orange-marmalade coffee cake two days later, a walnut muffin on Thursday and today a Draynut. The pastry was a combination of croissant and donut, and customers were lined up around the block to get their hands on the pricey dessert that her father had mistakenly referred to as a "dragnet."

Grace stared at her gold-rimmed plate, wondering if the pastry was as delicious as the food bloggers said it was. So far, she'd been impressed by the quality of the baked goods at Lillian's. She'd assumed the bakery wouldn't live up to the hype or her implausibly high standards. Trends came and went, and a little bit of buzz could go a long way when a business first opened. Grace was pleasantly—or rather unpleasantly—surprised to learn that yes, Lillian's was that good. She'd made the mistake of mentioning that to her father last night at dinner, and once again he'd urged her to return to the bakery to sample the rest of the items on the menu. Her father wanted to know exactly what the Draysons were producing, and expected her to report back about the inner workings of the family-operated bakery.

Reflecting on her mission, Grace considered what her dad wanted her to do. One week of spying and she was still uncomfortable about it. Sure, she wasn't doing anything illegal, but she felt like a snake for spying on the competition and wanted to stop. The biggest problem? Each day she returned to Lillian's brought her into close contact with Jackson—a man with soulful eyes, juicy lips she wanted to kiss and muscles she was dying to stroke. He was intelligent and perceptive, and Grace feared he'd catch on to what she was doing and expose her. Deep down, she was afraid of how attracted she was to Jackson and decided in her mind to ignore him—*if* he ever showed up at the bakery.

Grace glanced at her wristwatch again. She knew she should get going, but she didn't want to leave. Looking out the window, hoping to catch a glimpse of everyone's favorite baker, Grace couldn't believe how dark and gloomy it was. She couldn't remember the last time she'd seen the sun, and hoped the thick storm clouds held back the rain until she reached work.

"Rodolfo and I are abstaining from sex until our wedding night. Isn't that romantic?"

Grace swallowed the quip on the tip of her tongue. She'd asked her bestie, Bronwyn, to meet her at Lillian's for breakfast, but regretted it the moment their orders had arrived. When the speech pathologist wasn't cooing about her nectarine honey tart, she was gushing about her decades-older fiancé and their fall wedding. Slim, with hazel eyes and blond curls, Bronwyn exuded such warmth and confidence she made friends everywhere she went. "Yes," she drawled sarcastically. "It's the most romantic thing I've ever heard."

"You're just jealous. You *wish* you had a man as sweet and as loving as Rodolfo."

No, I wish *my vibrator wasn't on the blink, because it didn't get the job done this morning and I need an orgasm in the* worst *way!* Grace finished her coffee and set aside her mug. Anxious to sink her teeth into her dessert, she picked up her fork and cut into the Draynut. "Doesn't it bother you that Rodolfo isn't working?"

"No. I make enough money for the both of us and I love taking care of my Pooh Bear."

The fork slipped from Grace's hand and fell on the plate. Speechless, she stared at her friend in shock. Bronwyn liked to boast about all the nice things her fiancé did for her, but he was buying her expensive gifts with *her* charge card. Who did that? A real man would never take money from his woman, let alone demand a weekly allowance, and Grace didn't understand why her bestie was cool with supporting a grown-ass man.

"The economy's in the tank. People aren't buying luxury cars like they used to—"

"Then he should get a job at another dealership instead of mooching off you."

"No one's mooching off anybody. Rodolfo's a great catch, and I don't mind helping him out financially from time to time. We've had our ups and downs and even split up for a while, but I'd rather be with Rodolfo than anyone else. He's the only one for me…"

Listening to Bronwyn wax poetic about her fiancé, Grace realized she'd never loved anyone with unwavering devotion. Truth be told, she didn't understand men, couldn't figure them out, and doubted she ever would.

"Relationships are hard," she quipped, with a knowing look, a smirk sitting pretty on her lips. "*You* of all people should know that."

Grace ignored the dig, refusing to think about the night she'd dumped Phillip. To this day, Grace didn't know what had possessed her to date the loudmouth physical trainer. Her father had always warned her that men would be after her for her money, but she didn't believe him. Unfortunately, her dad was right. At the memory of the slap heard around the world—or rather inside Bronwyn's elegant Capitol Hill home—Grace groaned as if she was being physically tortured. "I don't want to talk about it. It wasn't my finest moment, and every time I think about it I want to hide. It's so embarrassing."

Bronwyn pushed a hand through her long, curly locks and Grace peered at her engagement ring. The diamond was so small she'd need a magnifying glass to see it, and the thick band looked cheap and old-fashioned. Grace was convinced Rodolfo had bought it at a pawn shop, or stole it from his great-great-grandmother, but she kept her thoughts to herself.

"Don't sweat it, slugger. Philip's face healed just fine."

Grace stuck out her tongue, then laughed when Bronwyn did the same.

"Hey, don't get mad at me. I'm not the one with the mean right hook."

"You're the worst, you know that?"

Bronwyn sobered. "If Philip apologized would you give him another chance?"

"No. Never. We have nothing in common, and we had no business dating."

"Rodolfo and I ran into him yesterday while shopping at Bellevue Square, and he said you're just taking a break, and you'll be an item again in no time."

"Ha!" Grace barked a laugh. "Girl, please, I'd rather join a convent!"

Bronwyn's shrill, high-pitched giggles drew the attention of the patrons seated nearby.

Hungry, Grace picked up her fork and put it in her mouth. Her eyelids fluttered closed as she savored the rich, sweet pastry. Tasting cinnamon and hints of nut-

meg on her tongue, she moaned in appreciation. The
dessert did not disappoint. Grace sampled another bite
of the Draynut and decided she didn't like the dessert;
she loved it.

"Tell me again why you wanted to meet here, and
not at the bakery?"

"My dad asked me to check out the competition so
here I am—"

"Sweet mother of God! Who is *that* and where has
he been all my life?"

Grace didn't have to turn around to know who Bronwyn was referring to, knew there was only one man
inside Lillian's of Seattle who could elicit such an em-
phatic response, but she did turn. Casting a glance over
her right shoulder, she caught sight of Jackson stalking
through the door, looking all kinds of sexy in a black
sports jacket, crisp slacks and leather shoes.

Grace couldn't take her eyes off of him. The man
was a force of nature, so freakin' hot her body tingled
in places that made her blush. He must have sensed her
watching him, felt the heat of her stare, because he met
her gaze. She wore an aloof expression on her face and
didn't react when he winked at her, but her heart was
doing backflips inside her chest. His grin revealed a set
of matching dimples, straight white teeth and a twinkle
in his eyes. Jackson moved with confidence, as if he
could have anything in the world—including her—and
that drew Grace to him.

"Do you know him?" Bronwyn asked. "Have you seen
him here before?"

"That's Jackson Drayson. He's one of the three owners."

"No," she quipped, her gaze dark with lust. "That's
my second husband!"

Grace cupped a hand over her mouth to smother her girlish laughter.

"You tricked me." Wearing an amused expression on her face, Bronwyn leaned across the table and leveled a finger at Grace. "You didn't ask me to meet you here so we could catch up. You came down here to drool over that tall, beautiful specimen of a man."

"As if. He's not my type—"

"Says the girl who's drooling all over her expensive designer dress!"

Grace noticed she wasn't the only person in Lillian's eyeing the dreamy baker. He'd captured the attention of everyone in the room and connected with patrons in meaningful ways. He shook hands, kissed babies, chatted with the group of senior citizens drinking coffee and saluted a female soldier waiting in line for her order. Jackson was a man's man, a woman's man, too, and it was obvious his customers loved him.

Watching Jackson charm everyone in the bakery made Grace realize her own inadequacies as an employee at Sweetness. She spent most of her days in her office, chained to her desk, and on the rare occasion she treated herself to lunch she sat outside in the park, not in the kitchen. Too many memories of her mother in there. Too many unfulfilled hopes and dreams, so she avoided the room at all costs. Customers, too. Everyone had a story to share about Rosemary, and hearing them broke her heart, overwhelmed her with pain and grief. For that reason, she kept her distance from the regulars.

"What's his story?"

Grace told Bronwyn what she knew about Jackson, which wasn't much, and noticed the expression on her friend's face morph from excited to skeptical.

"Single, fine and successful?" she drawled. "There *must* be something wrong with him."

"You mean besides that fact that he has a monster-sized ego?"

Bronwyn's giggles skidded to a stop and her eyes widened with interest as Jackson stopped at their table. "Well, hello."

"Good morning, ladies. Care to sample one of my Peppermint cheesecake bites?"

"Absolutely," Bronwyn cooed, helping herself to one of the round minicakes.

Stuffed, so full she couldn't move, Grace shook her head. "Nothing for me, thanks."

Bronwyn popped the dessert into her mouth, declared it was the most delicious thing she had ever tasted and stuck out her right hand. "I'm Bronwyn Johansson, and you're Jackson Drayson. I've heard a lot about you."

"Everything Grace told you is true."

Laughing together, Bronwyn and Jackson shook hands.

"It's true what they say. Beautiful women *do* travel in packs."

Bronwyn smiled so brightly she lit up the entire bakery. Grace tried not to gag. Surely, her friend wasn't impressed with his pickup lines. But, sadly, she was. Silent and wide-eyed, she couldn't believe her friend was flirting shamelessly with the bad-boy baker. Amused, Grace sank back in her chair and enjoyed the "Bronwyn and Jackson" show.

"You're a great baker," Bronwyn announced, her tone full of awe., "Your wife is one very lucky woman."

"I'm not married." His gaze slid across the table and landed on Grace. "But that could change any day now."

Heat singed the tips of her ears and flowed through her body. Jackson made her hyperventilate, caused her thoughts to scatter in a million directions, and there was nothing Grace could do to stop it.

"I haven't found Mrs. Right yet, but things are definitely starting to look up."

"Describe your ideal woman."

Grace kicked Bronwyn under the table, but her friend continued chatting a mile a minute.

"Don't be shy," she said, reaching out and patting his forearm good-naturedly, as if they were lifelong friends. "I love playing matchmaker, so let me help you find your soul mate."

Jackson rested the wooden tray on the table. "That's easy. I know exactly what I want."

"Do tell. Inquiring minds want to know."

"Bronwyn, don't encourage him," Grace implored, speaking through dry, pursed lips.

"I want to hear this. Go ahead, Jackson. I'm listening."

His stare was bold and raked over her body with deliberate intent. "She's five-ten, give or take a few inches, with mocha-brown skin, hourglass curves and legs like a Vegas showgirl."

Oh, my goodness, he's talking about me! Grace resisted the urge to cheer. Pride surged through her veins as she sat up taller in her chair. Fire and desire gleamed in his eyes, radiating from his chiseled six-foot body. Grace didn't speak, kept the leave-me-the-hell-alone expression on her face, but when Jackson flashed his trademark grin her heart smiled. It must have appeared on her face because he looked pleased with himself, as if he'd developed an antidote for an incurable disease.

He sat down in the empty chair beside her, and it took every ounce of her self-control not to kiss him.

"I know *just* the girl," Bronwyn said, vigorously nodding her head. "Want her number? It's 206-621—" Pop music played from inside her gold Michael Kors purse and she broke off speaking. Singing along with Taylor Swift, she retrieved her BlackBerry and checked the screen. "It's my Pooh Bear! Jackson, keep Grace company until I get back. I won't be long."

"My pleasure," he said, pouring on the charm. "Take your time."

Her breakfast forgotten, Bronwyn surged to her feet and strode off.

"You look amazing. Do you model for Gucci, or are you just a huge fan of their clothes?"

"Surely, there's someone else in here you can hit on," she said with a nod toward the cash register. "How about that cute young barista with the curly hair? She's always staring at you, and I'm sure she'd be flattered by your pickup lines."

"I don't spit lines. Just the truth."

Seeing her cell phone light up, she glanced down at the screen and read her latest text message. Of course. It was from her dad. He wanted to know how things were going, but Grace decided not to respond. Not with the enemy sitting so close.

"When are you going to let me take you out? You know you want to."

"I grew up here," she said, "so there's nowhere you can take me that I haven't been to a million times before."

"Try me. When we go out on Saturday night, I'll knock you off your feet. *Literally.*"

"Are you always this cocky?"

"Yes, as a matter of fact I am. I have reason to be. I'm a pretty cool dude!"

His facial expression tickled her funny bone. Grace didn't want to laugh, tried to swallow it, but it burst out of her mouth. Damn him! Why did he have to be funny and ridiculously hot?

"I love your laugh. It's as captivating as your smile."

"You wouldn't be flirting with me if you knew who I was."

"Ya think?" he said, leaning forward in his chair, his gaze full of interest. "Try me."

"I'm your worst enemy."

"Is that so, Ms. Nicholas? I prefer to think of us as colleagues, not rivals."

Grace choked on her tongue. Oh, hell no!

The fact that Jackson already knew who she was and had been flirting with her anyway made her mad, but more than anything she was disappointed. All this time, she'd thought she was pulling one over on him, but he'd been pulling one over on her! Swallowing hard, Grace reclaimed her voice and asked the question racing through her mind. "You know who I am? But I never told you my last name. How did you figure it out?"

"Google. Twitter. Facebook. There are no secrets in this day and age. A few clicks of my mouse and I knew everything I wanted to know about you…"

Jackson spoke in a tone so seductive her nipples hardened under her fitted teal dress, and her thighs quivered. It took everything in her not to crush her lips to his mouth and steal a kiss. The man was long, lean and ripped, and Grace imagined all of the delicious things they could do together. Dirty dancing. Skinny-dipping. Tantric sex. Stunned by her lascivious thoughts, she tore her gaze away from his face and took a moment to gather herself.

"I like the quote you posted on your Facebook page this morning and couldn't help wondering if it was about me. 'Don't be afraid of change. You may lose something good, but you may gain something infinitely better.'"

Everything in the bakery ceased to exist, faded to the background. Mesmerized, Grace listened to Jackson with growing interest, realized she'd been too quick to judge him. He was wise and insightful, and to her surprise she agreed with everything he said.

"There is no reason for us to be enemies. In fact, we could probably help each other. There is plenty of room for more than one bakery in town, and to prove it I'd be more than happy to give you a behind-the-scenes look at how things work at Lillian's."

His friendliness confused her. Why was he so willing to reveal company secrets?

"Come back after closing and I'll give you a tour of our state-of-the art kitchen."

Grace considered his offer. She suspected his invitation was the modern-day equivalent of inviting her upstairs to see his etchings, and wondered what *else* the hunky baker wanted to show her. The thought aroused her body, infected it with lust. *What's the matter with me? Why am I undressing him with my eyes? Why am I fantasizing about a man who has the power to break my heart* and *ruin my mother's business?*

"I better get back to the kitchen, or my sister will skin my hide." Standing, tray in hand and grin on display, he winked good-naturedly. "See you at seven o'clock, beautiful. Stay sweet."

Then, without waiting for her answer, he turned and strode off, as if the matter was decided. And that was when Grace knew she'd bitten off more than she could chew.

Chapter 4

Jackson kept one eye on the clock hanging above the kitchen door and the other on Mariah. His sister was flittering around the room, wiping counters, cleaning cupboards, rearranging spices and supplies—all in all ruining his plans. He couldn't cook a romantic dinner with Mariah lurking around, not without her asking a million questions, and if he didn't get rid of her ASAP the appetizers wouldn't be ready when his date arrived.

Jackson caught himself, striking the word from his mind. It wasn't a date. It was a business meeting, an opportunity to learn more about the enemy and her shop, Sweetness Bakery. It was Lillian's biggest competitor, the only thing standing in the way of greater profits and success. Jackson knew what he had to do. He had to get rid of the city's oldest bakery—and its titillating master baker with the gap-toothed smile and decadent, Lord-have-mercy curves.

Past conversations with his dad while golfing at
Rainier Country Club played in Jackson's mind as he
scrubbed the metal muffin tins soaking in the sink.
Graham had always admonished him to keep his friends
close, and his enemies closer—within striking distance—and he intended to take his dad's advice. There
was no way in hell he was going to let Grace and her
father outshine Lillian's of Seattle. He thought of telling Mariah about his numerous conversations with the
master baker, but sensed it was a bad idea. He'd tell her
tomorrow, after he'd successfully seduced Grace, and
would call Chase to bring him up to speed, as well.

"Things were so busy this afternoon I didn't get a
chance to tell you the good news," Mariah said, her
tone infused with excitement. "Belinda called at lunch
to tell me the Chicago clan is coming down for Bite of
Seattle."

Jackson twirled a finger in the air. "Lucky us."

"Jack, give them a break. They're trying to make
amends for the past and build relationships with us.
What more do you want them to do?"

"They think they're better than us because Lillian's
of Chicago blew up but we're every bit as good as they
are, if not better."

"I agree with you, but that doesn't mean we can't be
one big happy family."

Jackson was confused. He couldn't figure out why
his siblings, namely Mariah, wanted to be besties with
their snobby Chicago relatives. Over the years he'd
reached out to them numerous times—invited them
to his parents' anniversary bash, to come celebrate the
Christmas holidays and even offered to fly them to Seattle for a weekend—and even though they attended

family events Jackson still didn't feel close to them. And after the success of their "Brothers Who Bake" blog and bestselling cookbook, Carter, Belinda and Shari were busier—and snobbier—than ever. "What are you doing with yourself tonight?" he asked, wisely changing the subject. He didn't want to argue with Mariah, and talking about their relatives always put him in a bad mood. "Where is Prince Charming taking you?"

A girlish smile covered Mariah's face. "I don't know. Everett said it's a surprise, but I think he's treating me to a home-cooked meal, and I can't wait. He's an incredible cook."

"I'll finish up here. Go ahead and get your grub on," Jackson joked.

Instead of leaving, Mariah opened the closet and grabbed the wooden broom. "You've been here early every day this week, so if anyone should leave it's you, so go ahead."

"But it's almost six thirty. Aren't you going to go home and freshen up for your date?"

"There's no time. I'll just go straight to Everett's place from here."

"Dressed like that?" he asked, knowing full well his comment would get a rise out of her. "Okay, suit yourself, but don't say I didn't warn you."

Now he had Mariah's attention. She stopped sweeping, hitched a hand to her hip and fixed him with a dark, steady gaze. "Warn me about what?"

To buy himself some time, he turned the water on full blast and rinsed the dishes. Jackson didn't know what Everett had planned for his sister, but faked like he did. Mariah had to leave before Grace arrived, and if he had to fib to make it happen then so be it. "Maybe

Everett's taking you *out*." Jackson shut off the tap and dried his hands on his green apron. "Maybe he's taking you to Le Gourmand for a romantic dinner, then to the Usher concert."

Her eyes brightened, lit up like fireworks.

"Everett loves seeing you all dolled up, so go home, change out of those dirty clothes and put on your fanciest designer dress," he instructed. "Trust me. You'll thank me tomorrow."

Mariah squealed and Jackson chuckled. He'd never seen his sister so excited. Glad the pain of his sister's divorce was finally behind her, buried in the past where it belonged, Jackson made a mental note to thank Everett for taking good care of his sister when they played basketball on Wednesday.

"Does Everett have something big planned?"

"I don't know," he said shrugging his shoulders. "But what if he does? You don't want to be covered in flour when your man romances you, do you?"

Mariah untied her apron and tossed it down on the counter. "Good point."

"Have fun, sis, and tell Everett and EJ I said 'What's up.'"

The moment Mariah left the kitchen Jackson sprung into action. He had thirty minutes to cook and no time to waste. He was going to seduce Grace Nicholas, then persuade her to spill bakery secrets. The thought heartened him and a grin claimed his mouth. When he was through with the gorgeous master baker, she wouldn't know what hit her. Whistling along with the hip-hop song playing on the satellite radio, Jackson grabbed the bottle of bourbon he'd hidden under the sink and got down to work.

* * *

Grace sat inside her silver Jaguar XF, berating herself for driving to Lillian's after work instead of going
home. Eight hours after leaving the bakery, with Bronwyn in tow, Grace was back, and for the life of her she
didn't know why. Common sense told her to drive off,
implored her to stay far away from Jackson Drayson,
but she couldn't shake the feeling that tonight could be
a game changer. Maybe Jackson was right. Maybe they
could be friends...allies.

Raindrops beat against the windshield and a cold
chill flooded the car. The forecast called for heavy
rain, which should have been reason enough for Grace
to leave, but she didn't. Couldn't. Wanted to see what
Jackson had up his sleeve. Why he'd invited her back
to the bakery after closing. And if he was serious about
them working together, or just playing mind games, like
her ex. It was probably the latter, but Grace wanted to
know for sure.

*He invited you back here to put the moves on you.
Isn't it obvious?*

The thought should have scared her, should have
sent Grace running for the hills, but it didn't. Deep
down, she was attracted to him and flattered by his attention. Who wouldn't be? Jackson knew what to say
to make her smile, plied her with compliments, and
Grace looked forward to seeing the sexy baker every
morning. Truth be told, their flirtatious banter was the
highlight of her day, a welcome reprieve from her troubled thoughts.

Go home before it's too late, warned her inner voice.

Grace couldn't leave even if she wanted to. She'd
made the mistake of telling her dad about Jackson's

offer and he'd practically shoved her out Sweetness's doors at six thirty. He'd insisted she return to Lillian's, and although he was having dinner with friends tonight, he expected a full report tomorrow morning. Hell, he'd probably be sitting in her bedroom when she got home, champing at the bit for salacious gossip about their biggest competitor.

Thunder boomed and the wind howled, whipping leaves and tree branches around. The street was so dark Grace couldn't see where the bakery was. Was Jackson even inside? Had he changed his mind about meeting her, and left at closing? There was only one way to find out.

Twisting around, she searched the backseat for her belted trench jacket, but didn't find it among her things. *If I'd gone inside ten minutes ago instead of hiding out in my car, I wouldn't be stuck in the rainstorm now*, she thought, annoyed with herself for acting like a scaredy-cat.

Grace dug around in her Fendi purse for something to shield her from the rain. Picking up her cell phone, she noticed she had two messages from Phillip and snorted in disgust. She wasn't returning his call. What for? They were over and she had nothing to say to him.

Hearing a knock on the driver's side window, Grace glanced to her right. Standing in the street, holding an oversized umbrella, Jackson looked more like a knight in shining armor than her business rival. Drawn to him, Grace feared she'd be putty in his hands when they were alone, but willed herself to resist his seductive charms. She saw his lips move, heard his voice, but the rain was so loud she couldn't understand what he was saying.

"Let's go inside. Everything's ready..."

He gestured for her to come out of the car and stepped back to make room for her to exit the vehicle. Throwing open the door, Grace hopped out of her seat and took the hand Jackson offered. It was firm, felt nice around hers, and her heart smiled when he pulled her close to his side. Cold water covered her ankle-tie sandals and rain beat against her lace dress. The fabric stuck to her body like paint as they sprinted down the sidewalk and into the bakery.

Her eyes wide in surprise, a gasp fell from her lips. Grace was struck by how intimate the space looked, how sensual and romantic it was. The air held a savory aroma, potted candles filled the space with light and Bruno Mars was playing, singing earnestly about the woman he treasured. The table at the rear of the shop— the one they'd sat at that morning—was dressed in fine linen. Roses sat in a glass vase and a wine bottle was chilling in a bucket of ice.

"This isn't a date, is it?"

Radiating positive energy, his expression warm and welcoming, he spoke in an animated tone. "Of course not. I do this for all my customers, especially the ones who insult me!"

Jackson chuckled and the sound of his hearty laugh ticked her off. Grace couldn't think of a witty comeback and decided this would be her first and last visit to the bakery after dark. In a moment of weakness, she'd let her dad pressure her to return to Lillian's, but clearly, accepting Jackson's offer had been a mistake. *Why did I come here? What was I thinking?*

You weren't *thinking. You were lusting!* quipped her inner voice.

"I'm glad you're here." His husky voice broke into

her thoughts, instantly seized her attention. "I wasn't sure if you were going to show up."

"You didn't give me much choice," she teased, flashing a cheeky, good-girl smile. "I was afraid if I didn't come you'd hijack my Facebook page!"

Jackson stared at her, and Grace feared she had something on her face. Her heart raced, thumped so loudly she could barely hear the Luther Vandross classic now playing.

"I love when you do that."

His words confused her, caused a frown to crimp her dry lips. "Do what?"

"Smile," he said in a seductive whisper. "It dazzles me every time."

Grace tore her eyes away from his mouth. Determined not to cross the proverbial line, the one that could destroy her mother's legacy and dash her father's hopes and dreams, she inched back, out of reach. Jackson moved closer, boldly pursuing her. Her worries grew, intensifying like the storm raging outside. Aggressive, take-charge men were her weakness, and Grace feared if Jackson kissed her she'd fall into his arms and succumb to the needs of her flesh. Isn't that what she wanted? What she desired more than anything? To be ravished by this suave, debonair man who smelled of herbs and spices?

"I hope you're hungry, because I made all of your favorites."

"How do you know what I like? We've never gone out to eat."

His grin was sly. "Twitter, baby!"

"Of course. I should've known. Up to your old stalking ways, I see."

"A quick scroll through your posts revealed you love seafood almost as much as I do, so I made crab cakes, smoked salmon pinwheels, ginger-baked shrimp in pear sauce and some delicious desserts, as well. You're going to love it."

Grace felt her mouth drop open. Slamming it shut, she wondered if this was all a wonderful, amazing dream. Was this guy for real? Her ex had never cooked for her, but expected elaborate meals every weekend. Worse still, he was a homebody who'd rather watch CNN than wine and dine her. Jackson, with his out-going, down-to-earth personality, appealed to her, especially after the likes of Phillip "Bore Me to Death" Davies. Grace craved excitement, spontaneity, and her ex didn't cut it. She wanted to be with someone who spoiled her, who treated her as if she mattered more than anything in the world—a Renaissance man who cherished and adored her. Was that too much to ask? Apparently it was, because after countless blind dates she'd yet to find the man of her dreams.

"I'm glad you're here, Grace."

Jackson squeezed her hand, stroked her wrist with his fingertips, turned her on with each tender caress. Why did the gesture make her feel special? Desirable? Relationship advice her mother had given her years earlier echoed in her thoughts. *Do what feels right and you'll never go wrong.* Consumed with emotions—lust, hunger, desire and need—Grace decided to do just that, what she'd been fantasizing about doing to Jackson all week. Before she could stop herself she kissed him hard on the mouth. Crushed her body to his. Draped her arms around his neck, pulling him close. Licked his lips as if they were covered in chocolate. Touching his face, she inclined her head to the right and deepened the kiss. Encouraged by his groans, Grace slid her tongue into his mouth, boldly mated with his. And what a sweet, decadent treat it was.

Jackson pinned her to the wall, moving his hands down her shoulders, over her breasts, along her hips and thighs. It was too much. Had to be a dream. Couldn't be happening. Five minutes after arriving at the bakery they were French-kissing. How was that possible? Between kisses, Jackson told her she was sexy, how much he desired her, that he'd been thinking about her all day. His confession fueled her passion, made her want him, need him, even more. The magic and euphoria of his kiss was her undoing, causing her senses to spin and her body to tremble. His urgent caress made her nipples erect, her clit tingle and her panties wet.

An acrid odor polluted the air. Breaking off the kiss, her eyes flew open and her nose twitched. "Do you smell that?" she asked, peering over his shoulder.

Panic flickered across his face. "Shit! The appetizers!"

Whipping around, Jackson tore out of the room.

Grace followed him through the bakery, hoping and praying the kitchen wasn't on fire. Mad at herself for losing control, she inwardly berated herself for making the first move. *This is all my fault. I should have kept my hands to myself, and off of Jackson!*

Sprinting into the kitchen, Jackson swiped cooking mitts off the counter and slid them on without breaking his stride. In his haste to reach the stove, he knocked over the orange bottle beside the blender and it crashed to the floor. Glass flew in every direction, and the dark liquid pooled under the workstation. A strong, piquant

scent that made Grace think of cherries and warm caramel filled the air, and she knew it was bourbon. Spring-
ing to action, she grabbed the mouth of the bottle, tossed
it in the garbage can and searched the closet for a mop
and a broom.

Clouds of smoke billowed out of the oven. Waving
a hand in front of her face, Grace felt her eyes tear, but
she focused on the task at hand, on doing what she could
to help Jackson. Within seconds, the floor was swept,
mopped and gleaming.

One by one, Jackson retrieved the blackened baking trays and dropped them on the counter. The appetizers were so badly burned Grace couldn't decipher
what they were. A gray haze, thicker than LA smog,
engulfed the kitchen.

"Sorry about this. I feel like such an ass."

"No worries," she said with a small smile. "It can
happen to anyone."

"You must think I'm a total screwup."

His words—and his harsh tone—surprised her.
In that moment, Grace realized she'd pegged him all
wrong. Jackson was arrogant, sure, but he was also
kind, terribly sweet and sincere. Feeling guilty for causing the fire, and hoping to make amends, she leaned
over and gave him a peck on the cheek. "No way. Not
at all. You're a perfect gentleman."

His eyes smiled. "Why, thank you, Ms. Nicholas."

"It's the thought that counts, and you get an A for
effort."

And *for that amazing first kiss!*

"Really? An A for effort *and* another kiss?" Grin-
ning, he wiggled his eyebrows and glanced frantically

around the kitchen. "It's like that? Hold on. Let me burn something else!"

Grace burst out laughing. She couldn't believe Jackson was making light of the situation. Her ex would have thrown a fit, blamed her for ruining his dinner and sulked for the rest of the evening. Giving it more thought, Grace realized the fire never would've happened because kissing wasn't Phillip's thing—spending her money on frivolous crap was, but after she'd discovered the truth about him she'd dumped him and cut him out of her life. It hurt that he didn't love her, but Grace chose to focus on the present instead of the demise of their relationship.

"That was some kiss," he said. "Next time I'll make sure I turn off the oven before you arrive—"

"There won't be a next time." She fervently nodded her head. "It was a crazy, spur-of-the-moment thing that caught me off guard, but it won't happen again. It can't."

His face fell, but Grace didn't let his wounded expression stop her from speaking her mind. The kiss was a mistake and she wanted Jackson to know exactly where she stood, so there were no hard feelings later. "I'll admit it. I'm attracted to you," she confessed. His gaze was distracting, but Grace spoke with confidence, refusing to be sidetracked by his dreamy eyes. "We can't be friends, and we'll never be lovers—"

"Never say never. I've been told I can be quite persuasive." His grin was back in full force, weakening her resolve. "Let's start with dessert," he proposed, gesturing to the glass case at the rear of the room. "I made mint truffles, bourbon bread pudding and chocolate *stracciatella* cupcakes."

Her mouth watered and her stomach groaned. Grace

didn't know what *stracciatella* was, but she liked the way the word rolled off his tongue and wondered what else his tongue could do. Washing the thought from her mind, she fingered the hair at the nape of her neck, weighing the pros and cons of breaking bread with a man she found irresistible.

"Care to join me?"

Without hesitation, Grace said, "I'd love to." And she meant it. Hanging out with Jackson beat going home to an empty house, and she wanted to learn more about him and his successful family business. After all, that was the reason why she was here. To dig up dirt on the Draysons. To unearth their secrets. Back on her game, she fixed him with a seductive gaze and flashed her brightest smile. "Lead the way, Jackson. I'm right behind you."

Chapter 5

"Why aren't you married?"

Surprised by the question as they sat at the table eating their dessert/dinner, Grace picked up her glass and drank her tangerine cocktail to buy herself time. The drink was ice-cold, sweet and delicious, and she finished it within seconds. "Wow, talk about wasting no time getting into my business," she quipped, pointing her spoon at him. "If I wasn't starving and this bourbon bread pudding didn't taste like heaven, I'd be out of here."

"You can't blame me. Beautiful women usually have several boyfriends, and I don't want some muscle-bound jock busting in here, ready to beat me to a pulp for romancing his bae."

A giggle tickled her throat. "How many times do I have to tell you that I'm single?"

Jackson picked up the pitcher, filled her glass to the brim and Grace nodded her thanks.

"You didn't answer my question."

"No one's ever asked."

"Bullshit!" he argued. "You have 'wifey' written all over you and I find it hard to believe men aren't beating down your door to get to you."

"My focus is on the bakery, not finding Mr. Right. Not that I believe he exists. I don't."

He looked doubtful, as if he didn't believe her, and slowly stroked his jaw.

"This is crazy. We've only just met and here I am spilling my guts to you."

"No worries, bae. I'll send you my bill."

This time Grace couldn't stop it and a laugh fell from her lips.

"Most women your age are champing at the bit for an engagement ring."

"Not me," she quipped, dead serious. "Relationships are a pain in the ass."

"Care to elaborate?"

Tasting her cupcake, she decided it was divine and savored every delicious morsel. "Men are weird, complicated creatures and I don't have the time or the energy to figure them out. There are only so many hours in the day, and I'm a busy girl with a million things to do."

"It sounds like you've been dating the wrong men."

"Honestly, I don't get you guys," she complained, voicing her frustrations about the opposite sex, namely her ex-boyfriend. "You act like committed relationships are a death sentence, but you want all the perks and benefits of being my man. What's up with that?"

"You're overthinking things."

"Care to elaborate?" she said, posing the question he'd asked her seconds earlier.

"Men are simple. We only need three things to make us happy. That's it. Give us what we need and you'll have our heart forever."

"Is that so?" Skeptical but intrigued, she leaned forward in her chair, desperate to get the inside scoop on the opposite sex. *This is better than reading* Maxim *and* GQ, Grace decided, unable to control her excitement. She didn't have any guy friends, and since she didn't feel comfortable talking to her dad about her dating life she kept her questions to herself. Hearing Jackson's take on relationships was a treat. "Don't keep me in suspense. What are they?"

"ESPN, steak and mind-blowing sex."

Cracking up, Grace picked up her napkin and threw it at his face. "Now I see why you're still single. You're a handful and too slick for your own good!"

Thunder roared and lightning lit up the sky, but Grace was having such a good time with Jackson she didn't care about the havoc Mother Nature was unleashing on the city. Grace hoped her dad was home from dinner, and planned to text him before she headed home. Although she wasn't ready to leave the bakery just yet. Ready to talk for hours more she asked Jackson about his professional background. "Don't take this the wrong way, but you don't look like a baker."

"I get that all the time, but there's more to me than meets the eye."

"What were you doing before you opened Lillian's with your siblings?"

His deep, hearty chuckle filled the candlelit room.

"What *haven't* I done? I've been a bank manager, a business consultant, worked in real estate—buying and flipping commercial and residential properties—and I was even a professional poker player."

"Were you any good?"

"Google me."

Jackson winked and for the second time in minutes Grace laughed out loud. They'd been talking nonstop since they sat down at the table an hour earlier, and the more she learned about Jackson, the more she liked him. He was a character—loads of fun and sexy as hell, too.

"My winnings were enough to buy my dream car and a gorgeous home in Beacon Hill."

"Then why quit? Surely it was more glamorous than whipping up scones and éclairs."

Jackson parted his lips but didn't speak, then swallowed hard. He popped a truffle into his mouth, then washed it down with tangerine juice. "I got tired of the fast-and-furious lifestyle," he explained. "Every day was one big party, and soon I was spiraling out of control."

"When did you know it was time to walk away?"

"Last winter when I woke up in Amsterdam, hungover, disorientated and sick as a dog. Thanks to my family I got out of the game before it destroyed me."

Riveted, her ears perked up. Grace straightened in her chair, eager to hear more.

"Initially when Chase approached me about opening a bakery I laughed in his face, but once I spoke to my great-aunt Lillian and realized she had faith in us, I had a change of heart. I liked the idea of working with my siblings, and after Chase crunched the numbers and showed them to me, I jumped on board."

"Any regrets?"

"None whatsoever. I love this community, the shop and our customers, and most days I can't wait to get here and experiment in the kitchen." Jackson sighed, a wistful expression on his face as he glanced around the shop. "Life is a trip sometimes. After I quit poker and my engagement ended, I'd planned to go backpacking through Europe, but look at me now. I'm running a successful business with my siblings and, most shocking of all, I can actually bake."

Engagement? Speechless, the word rattled around in her brain. Grace wanted to know details, but Jackson changed the subject. Making a mental note to ask him about his former fiancée later, she answered his question about her favorite hobbies and interests. Nothing was off-limits—past relationships, stresses at work and sex—and his jokes put her in a playful state of mind. Jackson's eyes lit up when the conversation turned to travel. He spoke about the trip he'd taken to Barcelona with his father and brother last summer, vividly recounting the highlights of their two-week excursion.

"Do you have any vacation plans this year?" he asked.

Grace made her eyes wide, faking a bewildered look. "Vacation? What's that? It's been so long since I had one I can't remember what that is!"

"That's a shame. We'll have to remedy that, and the sooner the better."

His words, though spoken in jest, made her feel warm and giddy inside.

"Have you ever been to Fiji?"

"No, why?" she asked. "Trying to sell me your time-share?"

Jackson chuckled and the sound of his hearty laugh brought a smile to her lips.

"I'm going there in October for a few days. You should come and keep me company."

"Do you invite everyone you meet at Lillian's on vacation?"

"No, just smart, captivating beauties named Grace."

"You'd make a great politician," she joked, wagging an index finger at him. "You always know just what to say, and you're not only charming, but persuasive, as well."

"Does that mean you'll come?"

"No, it means I'll think about it. A lot can happen in four months."

Jackson nodded, then spoke in such a smooth voice her heart swooned. "You're right. We could end up eloping to Las Vegas and celebrating there."

"Or," she said with a laugh, "I'll go with my dad to London to check out an NBA pre-season game as planned. No offense, Jackson, but no one gets in the way of me and my favorite sport."

Happiness covered his face. "You like basketball? No way! Who's your team?"

"New York. They're going all the way this season."

"You wish. Me and four of my friends have a better chance of winning the NBA championship than your sorry, punk-ass team."

"Wanna bet?"

"Name your terms, Ms. Nicholas."

Grace wore a triumphant smirk. She knew Jackson would never agree to the wager, but she enjoyed teasing him. Hearing her cell phone buzz, she glanced down at the table. She had three new text messages from Bronwyn, but she decided to read them later. "A thousand-dollar donation to the winner's favorite charity."

"A thousand dollars? That's a lot of money."

"Put up or shut up," she quipped, an amused expression on her face.

"I'm in, but I also want a home-cooked meal as a part of the wager." Jackson wore a wry smile, took her hand in his and squeezed it. "It's been a long time since I had steak."

"Then I suggest you eat at your mother's house, because I don't cook. I bake."

No, you don't, whispered her inner voice. *You haven't stepped foot in the kitchen since your mom died, remember?*

He licked his lips. "No sweat. I'll teach you."

Thoughts of kissing him, of having her way with him, bombarded her mind, giving her goose bumps and heart palpitations. Earlier, she'd allowed herself to get caught up in the moment, and kissing him was the sexiest, most liberating thing she'd ever done.

"Did you go to culinary school?" Jackson asked.

"Yes, of course. You?"

"No. Seattle University."

"I graduated from the Seattle Culinary Academy, but everything I know about baking I learned from my mom—" Feeling her cheeks flush with heat and her throat close up, Grace broke off speaking and willed herself not to cry.

Jackson was mad at himself for upsetting her. Through his research, he'd read numerous articles about Rosemary Nicholas, the quiet, soft-spoken founder and proprietor of Sweetness Bakery who'd died last year.

Jackson couldn't take his eyes off Grace. He could see her inner turmoil, how the pain of her mother's unexpected death affected her, and admired her strength. Jackson didn't know what he'd do if something ever happened to his parents. Graham and Nadia Drayson were the heart and soul of his family and he couldn't imagine his life without them.

Gently caressing her hand, which was cradled in his, he spoke quietly, hoped his words would make her smile. "Your mom opened Sweetness Bakery when you were just a toddler. Did she immediately put you to work, or wait until you were out of diapers?"

Grace had the prettiest eyes and they twinkled as she spoke about her mother. Listening to her, Jackson was struck by two things—how much she loved her family and how knowledgeable she was about the bakery business. Grace knew her stuff, and became animated discussing the widely successful ads and promotions she'd done over the years with her mother's blessing.

"You've been baking your entire life," he pointed out. "Do you ever get sick of it?"

"I don't bake anymore. After my mom passed, I decided to take a break from the kitchen and help my dad manage the shop instead."

"Do you like crunching numbers?"

She nodded, but Jackson saw sadness flicker in her eyes and knew she was lying.

"How did I do? Did you enjoy your dessert/dinner?"

Her smile returned, blinding him with its warmth. "You knocked it out of the park!"

"I was hoping you'd say that."

"Everything was delicious, Jackson."

"I'm glad you approve."

"You're an amazing baker," she said, her tone filled with awe. "I'm sure your girlfriends love your culinary skills, but I bet your boys give you a lot of grief for working here."

"Not just my boys. My parents, too. My mom hates that my siblings and I opened a bakery, and thinks we should close up shop. According to Nadia, we're squandering the education she helped pay for, and embarrassing her and my father in the process."

"Does it bother you that your parents aren't supportive?"

Jackson shrugged. He couldn't bring himself to admit the truth out loud—not without sounding like a wuss—but it hurt that his parents thought he was a joke. Pushing his problems to the farthest corner of his mind, he returned to the conversation, giving Grace his full attention. He didn't want her to think he was bored. He wasn't. Far from it. He was enjoying himself immensely and couldn't remember the last time a woman had held his interest for this long. "Why did your last relationship end?" he asked, studying her over the rim of his glass.

"Holy moly! What's with all the personal questions?"

He met her gaze, heard her girlish laugh and felt ten feet tall. Making her smile gave him great satisfaction. Her sultry stare made his pulse soar and his heart raced faster than a Ferrari zipping down the freeway. "You're like a piece of baklava. Hard on the outside, but soft and fluffy in the middle, and I'm completely intrigued by you."

A smirk lit her lips. "Did you just compare me to a Turkish dessert?"

"I want to get to know you better—"

"Me, too," she said, cutting him off. "So, tell me more about your broken engagement."

Jackson coughed into his fist and shifted around on his chair. Mimi had betrayed him in the worst possible way and he had to forget her. He couldn't get his lips to work and struggled with his words for several seconds. "Mimi wasn't the woman I thought she was."

"I *told* you relationships were a pain in the ass!"

They laughed and nodded their heads in agreement.

"To friendship," Grace proposed, raising her drink in the air. "And decadent desserts!"

They clinked glasses and Jackson decided he was definitely seeing her again.

The niggling voice in the back of his head reminded him that Grace was the enemy, not an ally, but he ignored the warning. Tonight, she was sexy eye candy, the only woman he wanted to be with. Beneath her frosty facade was a fiery, spirited woman who'd been blessed with beauty and smarts, and he wanted to take her out on a formal date.

It was a wonder they hadn't met before last Friday. They ate at the same restaurants, enjoyed the same local bands and knew a lot of the same people. Their personalities definitely complemented each other, and they had so much in common the time quickly slipped by. Jackson liked her authenticity. Her honesty was refreshing and her girly, high-pitched laugh made him crack up every time.

"Gosh, this is good," she said. "I might have to steal the recipe when you're not looking."

Watching her devour her third mint truffle brought a grin to Jackson's mouth. He'd never seen a woman eat like Grace. She nibbled on each pastry and seemed to savor every bite, oohing and ahhing with more zeal than a game show audience.

A Lenny Kravitz song came on the radio and Grace danced around in her seat. Singing "American Woman" in perfect pitch she rocked her shoulders from side to side and snapped her fingers to the pulsing, infectious beat.

"Have you tried the Draynut yet?" he asked. "There's some in the fridge if you're interested."

"I got my hands on one this morning and it was amazing. I bet it's your best seller."

"No, actually our specialty cakes are and you'll never guess who makes them."

"What do you know about designing cakes?"

"Initially, nothing, so I watched online videos, got tips from my great-aunt Lillian and baked for hours every day. Fast forward two months and I'm busier than ever! On Sunday, I made a Lightning McQueen cake for a nine-year-old's birthday, on Tuesday I made a replica of the Holy Bible for a church appreciation luncheon and this morning I finished an elaborate cake for a Bollywood-themed wedding at the Four Seasons tomorrow."

"No way! Are you serious? What does it look like? How many tiers does it have?"

"I'd rather show you than tell you."

Jackson stood and came around the table. A month ago he'd been hired to make the wedding cake, and his goal was not only to impress the fortysomething couple tying the knot on Saturday, but also their four hundred guests. Excited to show Grace his latest design, he helped her up to her feet and pulled her to his side.

"Where are we going?"

"To see my newest creation, of course."

Taking her hand, he led her through the store, past the offices, kitchen and pantry, and into the cake storage room at the rear of the building. Jackson strode through the door and flipped on the lights. They flickered, cut in and out, and he made a mental note to change the weak bulb in the morning.

Spotting the covered wedding cake on the back table of the temperature-controlled room, Jackson felt a rush of pride. If someone had told him a year ago he'd quit playing poker and start designing specialty cakes, he would have accused them of being crazy. But here he was, doing just that, and making the bakery oodles of cash.

The door slammed shut and Grace yelped.

"Don't worry. It's not locked."

"So where's this one-of-a-kind, Jackson Drayson creation you've been bragging about?"

Whipping off the plastic cover with a flourish, he stepped aside and gestured to the gold-and-white cake with a nod of his head. "There it is. The Taj Mahal—"

Eyes wide, Grace gasped. Cupping a hand over her mouth, she glanced from Jackson to the wedding cake and back again. "Oh, my goodness! It's stunning!" she said, gushing, her excitement evident in her jubilant tone. "How did you make it? It must have taken you forever."

Grace had a million questions and he answered them all, taking the time to explain why he'd created the edible masterpiece. "The couple asked me to wow their guests, and since they grew up in Agra, India, I thought a Taj Mahal–shaped cake was the perfect choice."

"I'm blown away…"

Her words, like her lush red lips, were a turn-on.

"You weren't kidding," she continued. "There *is* more to you than meets the eye."

"Likewise, Ms. Nicholas. You're some kind of woman."

Jackson hooked an arm around her waist and pulled her right up to his chest.

"What are you doing?"

"Isn't it obvious?" His gaze zeroed in on her mouth. "I'm going to kiss you and it's going to be hot. Just like the first time."

Inhaling a sharp breath, she slanted her head to the right and stared deep into his eyes.

Jackson brushed his lips against her cheeks and over her delicate button nose, then slid his hands down her hips to grab her big, beautiful ass. Grace whimpered and clutched desperately at his T-shirt—it was all the encouragement he needed. He kissed her so hard on the mouth, with such hunger and passion, it stole *his* breath. He tasted bourbon on her tongue as it flicked eagerly against his own, and hints of nutmeg and cinnamon, too. His body ached for her, throbbed with uncontrollable need, and an erection rose inside his boxer briefs.

Overtaken by lust, his mind was bombarded with thoughts of sexing her, right then and there in the storage room, and Jackson fought the urge to do just that. To bend Grace over his work station, rip off her panties and take her from behind. If it wasn't their first time nothing would have stopped him from sexing her. Grace wanted him. That, he knew for sure. He felt it in her kiss, heard it in her moans and her urgent caress. Her hands were everywhere—buried in his hair, stroking his face, touching him through his shirt. Jackson nibbled on her bottom lip, licked the corners of her sweet, intoxicating mouth. "I've never wanted anyone as much as I want you right now," he whispered, shocked by his admission. "I have to get you out of this dress."

Her head fell back and Jackson placed soft kisses up her long, slender neck.

"Let's go to your place. It's closer."

Grace froze, her body tensed. "We can't."

"Why? Do you have roommates? Are they home right now?"

"No roommates, just an overprotective father who still treats me like a little girl."

Jackson disguised his disappointment by wearing a blank expression on his face. Second thoughts about hooking up with Grace flooded his mind. He didn't want trouble with her father and feared he was barking up the wrong tree. Then she gave him a shy smile, one that lit up her amazing brown eyes, and an electric shock zapped his body. He had to have her. Tonight. By any means necessary. Even if it meant breaking his rules and taking her back to his place.

"I live at home," she said, "and even though I have the basement all to myself my father would kill me if he came home and saw you inside my suite."

"Baby, no problem. I understand. We'll go to my crib instead."

"We just met. Furthermore, I'm not that kind of girl."

"Yes you are. You're a fun, gregarious woman who likes living on the wild side."

Grace laughed. "Hardly. I cover my eyes during thunderstorms and scary movies!"

"We won't do anything you don't want to do."

Dropping her gaze to her hands, she checked her gold watch.

Fearful she was going to turn him down, he said,

"I'm having a great time with you and I don't want it to end. We'll talk, listen to music and share a few more kisses. No pressure. I promise."

Unable to keep his hands off of her, he grazed his lips against her neck, nibbled on her earlobe. She made his heart rev, his mind spin, and one kiss wasn't enough. Would never be enough. Jackson was so busy devouring her mouth and stroking her supple flesh he didn't notice the light had gone out in the storage room until he opened his eyes and saw pitch-black darkness.

"Can we get out of here? This place is cold and dark and it's giving me the creeps."

Jackson couldn't see Grace's face, but he heard the apprehension in her voice, the fear. To reassure her everything was all right, he patted her hips and dropped a kiss on her cheek. Taking his cell phone out of his back pocket, Jackson pressed the power button and used the illuminated screen to find the door. He grabbed the handle and turned it. It didn't open. Puzzled, he scratched his head. "What the hell? This room is never locked."

"Let me try."

While Grace fiddled with the lock, Jackson moved around the small room, hoping to find a phone signal. "My cell doesn't get reception in here. Try yours."

"I—I don't have it," she stammered. "I left it on the table."

"Damn, I was hoping to call Mariah to come get us—"

"Are you telling me we're stuck in here? Trapped like damn mice?"

Grace lost it. Banged on the door. Screamed for help. Stomped her feet, then kicked off her sandals and threw them in frustration. "Don't just stand there!" she snapped. "If we're loud enough, someone walking by the bakery will hear us and call for help."

It wasn't going to happen, not with a violent thunderstorm raging outside, but Jackson knew better than to argue with her. To appease her, he banged on the door until his arms ached and his hands throbbed in pain. Reality set in, hitting him like a fist to the gut. They were stuck in the walk-in fridge and he had no one to blame but himself.

Chapter 6

The refrigerated storage room was a narrow space, smaller than a prison cell, and freezing cold now that they'd been there for four hours. Feeling a bitter chill stab her flesh, Grace rubbed her hands together and rocked back and forth on her sandals, which she'd put back on to warm her body. Her limbs were numb and her teeth were chattering so loud in her ears she couldn't think straight. She didn't have the mental fortitude to create an escape plan.

The display light on Jackson's iPhone illuminated the space, but the butterflies fluttering in her stomach intensified. Grace searched for a way out, staring in every nook and cranny for freedom. Metal shelves, as high as the ceiling, were stocked with bagged fruits, frozen pastry shells and an assortment of baked goods. The sweet, intoxicating scent in the air made Grace think of her mother. Rosemary grew fruits in their backyard, and as a child Grace used to pick raspberries and eat them straight off the bush.

"Grace, are you okay?"

Snorting, her lips pursed together in suppressed rage, she shot him a dirty look. "What do you think? I'm stuck in a cold, dark fridge, and no one knows I'm even here."

"Sit down. Let's talk. You can tell me more about Sweetness." Jackson put his cell phone on one of the shelves, sat down on the tile floor and crossed his legs at the ankles. "You might as well get comfortable. We're going to be here for a while."

"I—I can't stay in here," she stammered, willing herself not to cry, her voice trembling with fear and emotion. "I'll freeze to death, or die of asphyxiation!"

"Grace, calm down. You're yelling—"

"Don't tell me what to do."

"We're not going to die. It's a fridge, not a freezer..."

Her eyes narrowed, focusing on his face. Was he laughing at her? Making light of the situation? To regain her composure, she inhaled the fruity aroma in the room. It didn't help. The more she thought about her predicament, the more hopeless she felt, the more afraid.

"There's plenty of air in here and tons of food," he continued in a soft, quiet tone.

Pacing the length of the room, she racked her brain for the solution to her problem, because there was no way in hell she was spending the night in the storage-room fridge with Jackson. "I can't stay in here. I have things to do."

"Did you have another date lined up tonight?"

"This isn't a date. It's a business meeting."

"Do you kiss all of your business associates, or just me?"

Stumped, unable to think of a fitting response, Grace slanted her head to the left and hitched a hand to her hip. The next time Jackson said something smart to her, or flashed that stupid I'm-the-man grin, it was on. She'd had enough of his fresh mouth for one night.

"You don't strike me as the booty-call type."

"It's your fault we're even in this stupid mess," she grumbled.

"How was I supposed to know the door was locked? It's never locked."

"This wouldn't have happened if you weren't showing off."

Jackson pointed a finger at his chest. "You're blaming me for trying to impress you?" he asked, shock evident in his voice. "Have you looked in the mirror lately?"

Grace pretended his words didn't faze her, but inwardly her heart was dancing.

"You're stunning, in every sense of the word, and I'll do anything to make you smile, including showing off my one-of-a-kind specialty cakes."

And just like that, her anger abated, her expression softened and heat flooded her body. Jackson had a hold on her she couldn't explain, and it boggled her mind.

"Grace, hang in there. It will be five a.m. in no time and we'll be out of here."

"Ever the optimist," she said sourly, shaking her head. "I wasn't kidding when I said you'd make a great politician. You always know just what to say to smooth things over."

"I know," he teased, his face alive with mischief. "But I only use my powers for good."

"You think you're so cute—"

"I'm not? But my grandmother says I am!"

"God, you think everything's a joke, but it's not. This is serious. We're trapped!"

His gaze darkened and his jaw clenched, but Jackson didn't argue, didn't fight back.

Silence descended on the room, engulfed the space like smoke. They stood in silence for what felt like hours, but Grace didn't mind the quiet. She was glad to be alone with her thoughts, relieved to finally have some peace.

Tired of pacing, her feet sore, she sat down on the floor. Jackson was an arm's length away, and his spicy, woodsy cologne tickled her nostrils. Sleep pulled at her eyes, making her feel tired and weak. Grace thought about her dad, the mounds of paperwork on her office desk and her roller derby match on Sunday afternoon. Thinking about her teammates—her eleven sisters—made her smile. They'd been there when she needed them most, in her darkest hour, and Grace felt fortunate to have them in her life.

"Grace, I'm sorry. I know it stinks being in here, but it could be a lot worse…"

Really? Because I can't think of anything worse than being stuck in this fridge!

"I'll make it up to you," he continued. "Courtside seats to New York's season opener should do it, don't you think? I hate your team, but I love NYC, and since I know all the best places to eat, shop and play we'll party like it's 1999!"

"You'd fly across the country just to watch a basketball game?"

"Of course." Jackson nodded his head, wore a serious face. "Life is meant for living and I won't squander it, because tomorrow isn't promised to anyone."

"I guess that's one way of looking at it."

"Trust me, Grace, that's the *only* way of looking at it."

"Have you always had a laissez-faire attitude about life?"

His gaze dimmed and the smile slid off his mouth.

What was wrong? Grace wondered, scanning his face for clues. Why did he suddenly look so sad? So heartbroken? To lighten the mood and his spirits, she joked, "What do you do when you're not charming customers and whipping up Jackson Drayson specialty cakes?"

Jackson took such a long time to answer the question Grace was sure he'd missed it.

"I work out, play golf with my old man, hang out with my boys and coach basketball."

"No way!" she said, pleased to learn they had something else in common. "I played point guard for my high school and college teams."

"Were you any good?"

Grace winked. "Google me."

His dreamy grin knocked her for six, hitting her like an arrow to the heart.

"What grade do you coach?"

"I coach a wheelchair basketball team and we won the championship last year."

"Wow, Jackson, that's amazing! Congratulations," she said. "How did you get involved with the team?"

"In college, my roommate was struck by a distracted driver while walking to class," he explained in a solemn tone. "Diego was paralyzed from the waist down, but he never lost his zest for life or his love of sports.

Once I saw how much fun he was having in the league I wanted to get involved, so I offered to coach and the rest is history."

"How is your friend doing now?"

"Better than me!" Jackson chuckled good-naturedly. "He has a lovely wife, three great kids and a successful software business. Diego's living the American dream and I couldn't be happier for him. He deserves every success…"

Grace admired how open and honest Jackson was about his life. He spoke about his sheltered upbringing, his past mistakes and his disastrous dating history. His charity work and his dedication to his wheelchair basketball team impressed her the most. Jackson was a great conversationalist, by far the most interesting person she'd ever met, and although Grace was shivering like a nudist caught in a snowstorm, she was enjoying his company. "Wow, you have more layers than a *chocotorta*!" she joked, giving him a taste of his own medicine. "You strut around Lillian's like some badass baker, but you're actually a softie with a huge heart."

Their eyes met, zeroing in on each other, and desire singed her flesh.

"Did you just compare me to an Argentine chocolate cake?"

"Yes," she quipped, full of attitude. "You're welcome."

"You're a ballsy spitfire, and beautiful too…"

His voice tickled her earlobes, and south of the border. His piercing gaze made her mouth dry and scattered her thoughts. Memories of their first kiss filled her mind, causing her skin to tingle with desire, and

Grace wondered if he was thinking about their steamy lip-lock, too.

"Do you still play basketball?" he asked. "My rec team could use another point guard."

"Not anymore. I used to be on a coed team, but I quit once I joined the Seattle roller derby. I didn't have enough time to play both and once I started skating, I was hooked."

"No way. I don't believe you."

Grace rolled her eyes; she couldn't help it. Most people—namely her father's snotty society friends at the country club—were shocked and appalled to learn Grace played such a rough, physical sport, so Jackson's reaction didn't surprise her. "Looks can be deceiving," she reminded him, recalling their conversation during dinner. "You of all people should know that. After all, you are a former poker player turned baker who coaches wheelchair basketball."

"You're a roller derby girl? Get out of here. Seriously?"

Oozing with confidence, Grace nodded and pointed her thumbs at her chest. "My nickname's Lady MacDeath and I'm the lead jammer for the Curvy Crashers. We compete all over the country and finished third in our division last season. This year, we have a shot of winning it all, and we will. You just wait and see."

"Damn, I never would have guessed it. You're so soft and delicate."

"There's nothing *soft* or *delicate* about me."

Jackson raised his hands in the air. His expression was contrite and his tone was remorseful. "Grace, I didn't mean to offend you—"

"Just because I grew up in the suburbs doesn't mean I'm a wallflower. I'm not. I'm strong and tough and I have a mean right hook, so don't mess with me."

He chuckled and told her he'd never dream of it. "When's your next match? I want to come."

"Why? So you can make fun of me?"

"No, so I can cheer you on. In case you haven't noticed I have a sweet spot for smart, captivating beauties who aren't afraid to speak their minds." He added, "And that's you."

Sitting motionless, transfixed by the intensity of his gaze, Grace imagined herself kissing him and ripping his clothes off his body. Shivers spread from the tips of her ears to her toes. His smile stirred her senses, made her brain short-circuit and her limbs shake uncontrollably. To conquer her explicit thoughts, Grace pressed her eyes shut and rested her head against the wall.

"You're cold." Jackson moved beside her, slid his arms around her shoulders and held her tight. "I'm not putting the moves on you. I just can't stand to see you shiver…"

Too tired to argue, Grace snuggled against him, relishing the feel of being in his arms. His touch was needed, welcome, and his clean, refreshing cologne helped soothe her mind. Dozing off, Grace couldn't help thinking, *I wish you* were *making a move!*

Jackson glanced down at his cell phone, checked the time and sighed in relief. Mariah would be at the bakery within the hour and this bizarre ordeal would finally be over. So much for keeping his plan under wraps. Mariah would have a million questions about

Grace, and if Jackson wanted to keep his life—and his job—he'd have to tell his sister the truth.

Grace stirred beside him, murmuring softly in her sleep, and Jackson tightened his hold around her. Pulling her close to his chest, he shut his eyes and inhaled her soothing lavender scent. He liked feeling her body against his, imagined them naked, moving together as one, and desire scorched his flesh. Jackson touched her hair, tenderly caressed her neck and the enticing curves of her hips. He wanted Grace, could almost taste her kiss, but he feared she'd spurn his advances. And for good reason. He'd blown it last night, messed up. Everything that could go wrong had, and he blamed himself for their current predicament. Hell, he'd screwed up the moment Grace had arrived. He'd burned the appetizers, knocked over an expensive bottle of bourbon that splashed onto her designer clothes and, if that wasn't bad enough, they'd been forced to spend the night in the storage-room fridge. After their wild, crazy night Jackson wouldn't be surprised if Grace never wanted to see him again. He'd messed up royally, but was determined to make it up to her.

He considered their night together. Yeah, they'd yelled and bickered, even insulted each other, but as far as Jackson was concerned it was water under the bridge. Grace had captured his attention the moment they'd sat down to dinner. She was so energetic and fascinating that he'd committed everything about her to memory. She loved jazz music, had dreams of relocating to New York, was addicted to raisin bagels and coffee and spoke Spanish fluently. Added to that, she had a blinding white smile and the best pair of legs in the city.

Jackson lowered his mouth to hers. He couldn't help

it. He cautioned himself to pull away, before he lost control, but her eyes fluttered open and she returned his kiss. It was filled with passion and hunger. Grace didn't speak, didn't need to. She communicated what she wanted with her lips, tongue and hands.

The light from his cell phone illuminated the sparkle in her eyes, the smirk on her lips and her come-hither expression. Sliding onto his lap, Grace grabbed his shirt collar, yanked him forward and mated desperately with his tongue. *Hot damn!* His body hardened and an erection grew inside his pants. Grace was ballsy and aggressive and Jackson loved it, loved not knowing what to expect next. She stroked his neck, slid her delicate hands down his shoulders, turned him out with each flick of her tongue against his ear. Did it ever feel good. Her moans consumed the air, exciting him, making him want her even more.

Jackson undid the buttons on her dress. Surprised to see a butterfly tattoo painted above her right breast, visible through her white push-up bra, he kissed it, then drew his tongue along the intricate design. He couldn't stop kissing her, licking her, stroking her warm, sweet flesh.

Arching her back, she swayed her body to an inaudible beat. Grace told him how good it felt, how much she desired him, and begged for more. He couldn't believe this was the same woman who'd given him the cold shoulder days earlier, who'd adamantly refused to give him her phone number. "Damn," he breathed, nibbling on the corners of her lips. "I want you, Grace, God knows I do, but not like this. Not in the fridge inside my family's bakery."

"Slow your roll, Jackson." Her eyes were bright, alive

with warmth and humor. "We've only known each other for a week. What kind of girl do you think I am?"

"The spontaneous type who enjoys breaking the rules and living in the moment."

Desire was etched on her face, seeped into her sultry tone. "Only time will tell."

"Your beauty boggles my mind, you know that?" Nuzzling his nose against hers, then along her bare shoulder, he playfully cupped her ass in the palms of his hands, rubbing and squeezing it. Desperate for her, it took everything in him not to free his erection from his pants and plunge it deep inside her sex. "I'm glad you don't have an Instagram account."

"Why? Afraid of a little healthy competition?

"No, because your smile's so beautiful it would break the internet!"

Grace laughed and Jackson decided it was the loveliest sound he'd ever heard.

Chapter 7

"I wish we were at my place." Jackson brushed his mouth against her ear. "I'd carry you into my master suite, give you a champagne bath, then make love to you…"

Grace sucked in a deep breath. *Oh, my. Yes! Take. Me. Now!* Delicious shudders racked her body, prickling her skin with goose bumps. Jackson spoke in a low, seductive tone that made her skin tingle and her panties wet. His gaze slid down her curves, boldly assessing her, turning her on like only he could. It had never been like this. No one had ever made her feel this way before—desperate, ravenous—and Grace didn't know how to regain control.

His mouth, on hers, put her in an amorous mood, and nothing else mattered but pleasing him. The magic and euphoria of Jackson's kiss weakened her resolve, stole every rational thought from her mind, and Grace knew they were going to have sex on the storage-room floor. At the thought, every nerve in her body quivered.

Grace inhaled his scent, drank in his cologne, fighting the urge to rip the clothes off his body. Her hands had a mind of their own. She touched and caressed his face, his shoulders, and stroked his six-pack underneath his T-shirt.

Overcome with desire, Grace did what she'd fantasized about doing all week—she kissed Jackson passionately, fervently, and it felt amazing. Feeling his hands on her breasts, cupping them, kneading them, teasing her erect nipples with his thumbs, she hoped they'd dive between her thighs to play there, too.

Light flooded the room and high heels slapped violently against the floor.

"Jack, is that you? What the hell is going on in here?"

Grace froze. Startled, her eyes flew open and she jumped to her feet. Squinting to see who'd barged inside the storage room, she dropped her hands to her side and studied the new arrival in the handkerchief-hem blouse and skinny jeans. Grace wondered who the petite beauty was, and why she was yelling at Jackson. Her stomach clenched, then dropped to her feet. Was the woman his girlfriend? Grace gulped. Were they serious? Did he love her?

"Thank God you're here," Jackson said. "Are we ever glad to see you."

Confused, she gave Jackson a sideways glance. *We are?* Staring down at her clothes, she was shocked to see her push-up bra on full display. She did up the buttons, straightened her dress and stuffed her feet back into her sandals. Grace didn't have to look in the mirror to know her appearance was frightening. Day-old makeup, wrinkled clothes, wild, messy hair. It was a wonder the woman didn't spin around and run screaming from the room.

"What's going on? Why are you in here playing tonsil hockey with this skank?"

"Excuse me?" Grace cocked her head, glaring back at the stranger. *Who was she calling a skank?*

"Mariah, relax. It's not what you think. This is my friend Grace." Nodding, Jackson clasped her hand and wore a broad, reassuring smile, one that caused her anger to dissolve. "Grace, this is my sister."

Sighing inwardly, Grace felt the tension leave her body. *Thank God.* She liked Jackson and wanted to get to know him better, but not if he was dating every woman in Seattle. Grace was annoyed his sister had insulted her earlier, but she decided to take the high road, and smiled politely. "It's wonderful to meet you, Mariah. I've heard a lot about you."

"I can't say the same."

"I brought Grace in here to show her the fondant cake I made for the Chakpram wedding and we got locked inside," Jackson explained. "Needless to say, it's been one hell of a night."

Mariah adamantly shook her head. "That's impossible. The door's never locked."

"Crazy, I know, but we've been stuck in here for the past six hours."

"I'm *sure* you made good use of your time."

Mariah gave her a disgusted look, and Grace wished the ground would open and swallow her up. How much had Mariah seen? Had she seen them pawing each other? Heard them groaning? Grunting?

"I tried to call for help, but my cell doesn't get reception in here."

"Jack, you shouldn't have been back here to begin with. The storage room is for supplies, not late-night booty calls."

"Mariah, you're way out of line. It wasn't like that."

"Yes, it was. With you it *always* is."

"It won't happen again."

"Sure it won't," she grumbled, giving him her back.

Jackson walked up behind his sister, shifted her around and gave her a loud, wet, kiss on the cheek. Mariah giggled and swatted his shoulder. "Cut it out." Her voice was stern, but her eyes were smiling. "You're going to ruin my makeup and Everett's coming by later for lunch."

"I'm going home to shower and change. I'll be back in a few."

"Please hurry. Kelsey called in sick again and Nita doesn't start until ten o'clock."

"No worries, sis. I'll be back before you know it."

The siblings embraced and Grace decided it was the perfect time to make her getaway.

"It was nice meeting you, Mariah. All the best with the bakery."

"Grace," she said tightly, her tone colder than the storage-room fridge.

Anxious to leave, Grace marched out of the room, past the offices and down the hallway. The music was still playing in the bakery and if not for her sour mood she would've laughed at the irony of the situation. Pharrell was chirping about how happy he was, his vocals suffused with joy and cheer, but Grace was pissed, so wound up her body was shaking for all the wrong reasons. Mad at herself for getting caught in the act with Jackson, she swiped her things off the table and dropped her cell phone in her purse. Desperate to make a hasty getaway, she sped through the bakery and burst through the front door. The sooner she got away from Mariah and her ugly attitude, the better.

Hazy and covered with clouds, the morning sky looked somber and bleak, but Grace had never been so relieved to be outside. Putting on her sunglasses, she inhaled the crisp, warm air.

"Grace, wait! Hold up! I'll walk you to your car."

Hearing Jackson's voice, Grace stopped and glanced over her shoulder. At the sight of him, her mouth dried and her heart stopped. God, he was dreamy. She couldn't look at Jackson without thinking about sex, and wanted him now. Could almost taste his kiss, and his gentle caress. Even though she'd insulted him, he'd taken great care of her last night and she'd never forget how special he made her feel. And what an amazing kisser he was. If not for Mariah busting into the storage room, they probably would have made love on the floor. The thought made her girly parts tingle and goose bumps flood her skin.

"Sorry about that."

Jackson slid a hand around her waist and hugged her possessively to his side, as if they were a couple in a loving, committed relationship. The gesture made her feel cherished, cared for, and though she tried she couldn't wipe the lopsided smile off her face.

"Mariah didn't mean any harm—"

"Is that why she called me a skank?"

"Don't take it personal. She didn't mean anything by it."

Grace couldn't stop from rolling her eyes.

"Mariah came in this morning, found the bakery a mess, couldn't reach me on my cell and was shocked to find us kissing in the storage room."

His explanation made sense, as did his sister's behavior, but her run-in with Mariah had left a bitter taste in her mouth and Grace didn't care if she ever saw his sister again. Troubled, she asked the question at the forefront of her mind. "Are you seeing anyone?"

"You mean besides you? Why date around, when I can have the sexiest woman alive?"

He drew her into his arms, held her tight.

"You'll be in later, right? What time?"

"No, my days of spying on you are over."

"They are?" He sounded disappointed and surprise colored his cheeks. "Really?"

"Jackson, I'm sorry," she said, overcome with guilt and shame. "I never should have done it in the first place. I don't know what I was thinking."

"Apology accepted. I probably would have done the same thing if I were you." He shrugged, wore an impish smile. "Actually, I have. Poker is a cutthroat game and sometimes to win you have to play dirty."

Grace wanted to know more about his past, but before she could ask the question running through her mind, Jackson spoke. Mesmerized by his husky tone, she couldn't concentrate on what he was saying. The man was a perfect ten. Boyish grin, hot body, smart, confident and romantic, he was everything a woman could want.

"I'm taking you out tonight," Jackson announced.

Remembering the last time she'd heard those words, her body tensed.

"We can go anywhere you want. Canlis. Metropolitan Grill. El Gaucho." Jackson winked and affectionately patted her hips. "New York City."

A smile tugged at her lips, threatened to explode across her mouth, but Grace kept a straight face. She couldn't risk losing her heart to a man who'd never commit to her, so it was imperative she keep her distance. "I don't think we should make seeing each other a habit."

"Why not?"

"Ask your sister."

"We'll talk tonight. What time's good for you?"

"I have plans with my dad." It was a lie. She had nothing to do besides wash her hair, but Grace didn't want to hurt his feelings. They'd had a great night together, filled with tons of laughs, interesting conversation and scorching French kisses, but they could never be more than friends, so why bother? Why risk her heart for a man incapable of love and commitment?

"Tomorrow then," Jackson said, as determined as ever to get his way. "We'll have Sunday brunch, then spend the rest of the day exploring this great city."

"I can't. I have a game at five o'clock."

"Even better, we'll have a victory dinner at Palisade fit for a roller derby queen." Jackson touched her face, drew a finger against her cheek. "Please don't shoot me down again. I don't think my ego could take it. I'm enthralled by you, Grace, and I don't care how long it takes. I'll make you mine."

Stunned—and aroused—by his declaration, all Grace could do was stare at him. She couldn't catch her breath and struggled to find the right words. Didn't have any. Couldn't think of anything to say. Grace wanted to see Jackson again, loved the idea of having a romantic dinner with him, but she didn't want to go to the most expensive restaurants in the city. If they did, word could get back to her father, and he'd kill her for publicly breaking bread with the enemy. "I'll have dinner with you next weekend," she said quietly, loving how his hands felt on her skin, how her body responded enthusiastically to his touch.

"I don't think I can wait that long."

Grace laughed. "You'll survive."

"Seven days sounds like an eternity."

You're right. It does. But I have to be smart about this. I don't want to get hurt again.

"Can we go somewhere less popular?" Grace asked. "If we go to Palisade there's a good chance I'll run into someone I know and that would be a disaster."

Jackson nodded his head, gave her a sympathetic smile. "I understand."

"You do?"

"Honestly, I don't care where we go as long as we're together." He cupped her chin in his hands, gave her a pensive look. "I'll pick you up next Saturday at seven o'clock sharp—"

"No!" Her voice was loud, filled with panic. "Let's meet here. It's safer that way."

"You don't want me to meet your pops? Why? Are you ashamed of me?"

"No, of course not, but no one can find out about us. My father would kill me if he knew about last night, and with everything going on at the bakery I don't want to add to his stress."

To smooth things over, she reached up on her tiptoes and gave him a peck on the lips.

"I won't tell a soul. It will be our little secret."

"And Mariah's," she quipped.

"I'll talk to her. Don't worry."

"Thanks, Jackson. That means a lot to me."

"Wear a short red dress for our date," he instructed, brushing an errant strand of hair away from her face. "I love the color on you, and your long legs, as well."

"I'll see what I can do."

"You better, or you'll never have my bourbon pudding again."

Grace widened her eyes and clapped her hands to her face. "Oh, no!" she wailed in an anguished voice. "Not the bourbon pudding! Whatever will I do?"

Jackson cracked up and Grace laughed, too.

The sun crept over the horizon, lined the sky with brilliant shades of yellow, orange and pink, and Grace knew if she didn't hurry she wouldn't have time to change before work, and if she showed up at Sweetness in the same outfit she wore yesterday, her dad would put two and two together and there'd be hell to pay. "We'll talk later." She unlocked her vehicle with the keyless remote, and as the headlights flashed and beeped she hurried toward it. "See ya!"

"You drive a Jaguar XF?" Jackson asked, gesturing to her car with a nod of his head.

"It was my mother's car. I'm more of an SUV girl, but it's growing on me. Why? Do you have a problem with the brand?"

"Not at all. In fact I have the exact same car, except mine has tinted windows…"

Following his gaze, Grace spotted a black Jaguar XF parked across the street under a lamppost and laughed to herself. *Wonders never cease,* she thought, reading his personalized license plate. "'Bigshot,' huh?" she teased, wiggling her eyebrows. "How fitting."

"I think so. Why be mediocre when I can be the best?"

Jackson opened her car door and Grace slid inside. Taking her cell phone out of her purse, she noticed it was dead and plugged it into the charger.

"Speaking of the best, I need your phone number. How am I supposed to sweep you off your feet if we don't talk every night for hours on end about how perfect you are?"

Amused, Grace rattled off her cell number while putting on her seat belt.

"Drive safely, beautiful. I'll call you later."

"I will. Thanks for everything, especially dessert. It was delicious."

"Are you talking about me, or my pudding?"

Grace laughed, told him he was crazy and put the key in the ignition. As she turned to wave goodbye, Jackson captured her lips in a kiss. Warmth spread through her body, scorching her skin with fire as his tongue boldly claimed her mouth. Fighting the urge to pull him into the car and pick up where they'd left off in the storage room, Grace braced her hands against his chest and broke off the kiss. "Bye, Jackson."

Reluctantly, Jackson stepped onto the sidewalk. He watched the Jaguar cruise down the street, turn left at the intersection and disappear out of sight. Damn, what a night. He'd spent it with an angel and wanted to reunite with her tonight. There was no way in hell he was waiting until next Saturday. Screw that. He'd make an impromptu visit to Sweetness if he had to, because seven days without seeing Grace would be torture.

Turning toward the bakery, he spotted Mariah in the front window and released a deep sigh. He contemplated jumping in his car and driving off, but decided better of it. No sense making a bad situation worse. Besides, he wouldn't get far. His sister was pissed, no doubt about it.

Her arms were folded across her chest, her eyes were dark with anger and if looks could kill he'd be six feet under the ground.

Chapter 8

"Which team is Grace on?" Diego asked. "What position does she play? Is she any good, or just eye candy?"

Grace Nicholas isn't just eye candy, Jackson thought, his chest puffed up with pride, his smile bright enough to power the entire Seattle roller-skating rink with light. She was infinitely more. *Grace is, hands down, the smartest, most appealing woman I've ever met, and I want her bad.*

"How long has Grace been a roller derby girl?"

"Beats me." Jackson sat down in the seat beside Diego's wheelchair, and handed him an ice-cold beer. The arena was filled with fans, reeked of sweat, cheese nachos and cotton candy, and the drunken women seated behind him giggled as they sang off-key. It wasn't Jackson's scene, but since Grace was in the building and he wanted to surprise her, he'd stick it out until her match was over. "If we didn't hear about this game on the radio, I would have missed it. I spoke to Grace last night, and twice today, but she didn't mention her big match."

"You know why, right?"

"No, but I'm sure you're going to tell me."

"It's obvious," he said smugly, his raised eyebrows crawling up his forehead. "Grace didn't invite you to her game because she didn't want to risk you running into her *real* boyfriend. I don't blame her. You're not exactly a catch…"

Jackson didn't speak, but the murderous expression on his face must have terrified his buddy because Diego bumped elbows with him in an attempt to smooth things over.

"Relax, man. I'm just playing. Everyone knows roller derby chicks love bakers!"

Diego chuckled, guffawed as if he was watching an HBO comedy special.

"No offense, bro, but your career sucks." He snorted and shook his head as if he was scolding his five-year-old son. "Quit playing Martha Stewart and get a real job. A *man's* job."

His best friend had been teasing him ever since they'd left the house, but Jackson knew what to say to shut him up. "Diss me one more time and you're uninvited to Chase's bachelor party next month. Now, *that's* funny!"

Panic flashed in his eyes. "We always joke around," he argued, raking a hand through his short brown hair. "We're boys. That's what we do. When did you get so touchy?"

When the woman of my dreams walked into my fam-

ily bakery and turned my life upside down. Startled by the realization, Jackson deleted the thought from his mind and picked up his beer. It had been a week since Freezergate—what Grace jokingly called the incident in the storage room fridge—but it felt like months had passed since the ordeal. They'd seen each other every night, and their secret affair was not just thrilling, but hot. Some nights Grace came to his place for dinner, one night they went dancing and out for drinks and yesterday they'd both played hooky from work and drove the eighty miles to nearby Ashford, Washington.

His thoughts returned to yesterday and a grin claimed his mouth. To impress her, he'd planned several fun-filled activities and romantic surprises. They'd kicked off the day with a two-hour food tour that took them from one delicious restaurant to the next, then enjoyed a massage at the best spa in the city, but the highlight of the day was boating along Mineral Lake. The sky was clear, the weather perfect, and Grace was warm and personable. They'd talked and laughed, kissed under a curtain of stars, and by the time they returned home Jackson was so hot for Grace he couldn't think about anything but making love to her.

"Don't do anything stupid like fall for her," Diego warned. "Grace works for the competition, and Mariah and Chase will kill you if you hook up with her. Don't do it, man."

Jackson tuned him out and kept his eyes open for Grace, searching the arena hoping to catch a glimpse of the brown-eyed beauty. At home, watching TV earlier, he'd texted Grace so many times Diego had accused him of being sprung. Jackson didn't mind his buddy poking fun at him—he didn't give a rat's ass what he thought.

Grace was special to him, more important than any other woman in his life, and he wanted her to know he was thinking about her when they were apart. Add to that, they had incredible chemistry. Jackson had needs, insatiable sexual desires, and something told him the roller derby beauty with the luscious lips and banging body could make his fantasies come true.

"Introducing the Curvy Crashers!" the female announcer shouted, her voice slicing through the noise in the packed stadium. "Make some noise for Lady MacDeath!"

Jackson surged to his feet and pumped his fists in the air. Cheering louder than anyone, he watched as the Curvy Crashers took to the rink, smiling, waving and blowing kisses to their fans. Grace looked tough but sexy in her purple starred helmet, fitted tank top and itty-bitty black shorts. The number 49 was written on her cheeks, her makeup was eye-catching and her fishnet stockings drew his gaze down her thighs and legs. He followed her around the rink, tracked her every move, thoughts of making love to her dominating his thoughts.

"Who's Grace?"

"Number forty-nine."

Diego whistled. "Jack, you were right. She *is* stunning."

"She's also fun, sophisticated and ridiculously smart," he said, his heart filled with pride.

"Start an I-Love-Grace fan club," he joked. "You're damn near blushing!"

The teams found their place at the start line, the referee blew the whistle and they were off. Roller derby was high-energy, loud and physical, and Jackson loved everything about it. The noise, the hits, how tough and competitive the players were. The crowd was wild, the air was charged with electricity and the excitement was palpable. Flying around the track, Grace showed off her incredible agility, strength and speed. Hectic and fast-paced, there was a lot happening on the track—players fighting, pushing and falling on top of each other—but Jackson kept his eyes on Grace, blocked out everything else in the vicinity, and focused his gaze on her pretty face.

"Man, this game is intense."

"You're telling me," Jackson agreed, blowing out a deep breath. "They've only played fifteen minutes, but I'm sitting here sweating bullets and we still have another period to go."

"How do they score points?"

"Hell if I know! I'm a roller derby virgin just like you."

Diego took his iPhone out of his jacket pocket and accessed the internet. "Thank God for Google."

The men chuckled and bumped beer bottles.

"I remember Grace mentioning that she was the lead jammer for her team, whatever that means, but I have no clue how the ref is calling the game, or how the teams earn points."

"'Each team puts five players out on the track. One jammer, one pivot and three blockers,'" Diego said as he slid his index finger across the screen. "'The lead jammer is the only person who can score, and does so by passing the skaters on the opposing team.'"

Listening to Diego read the rules of the game, he realized Grace was the only person on her team who could score, and cheered when she crashed into an opposing player, and the buxom blonde fell to the ground.

Decked out in elbow, wrist and knee pads, Grace looked ready for combat, and watching her fight to the lead of the pack made him wonder what kind of lover she was. Was she expressive in bed? Passionate? Erotic? Down for whatever? They hadn't made love yet, but remembering their X-rated make-out session in his car last night as they were parked on a secluded area on Highland Drive gave Jackson an instant erection. He desired her more than anything, but he sensed she wasn't ready to take their relationship to the next level, and Jackson didn't want to pressure her to have sex. Grace was worth waiting for, and he knew when they finally made love it was going to be incredible. Just like her kisses.

Jackson heard his cell phone chime, read his newest text message and smiled. Chase was checking up on him, and wanted to know how he was doing. Jackson missed his brother and wished he was back from his trip with Amber. If Chase was around he'd have someone to vent to, because talking to Diego was out of the question. His friend was in a sour mood, upset because he was at odds with his wife, and his negativity was depressing. Mariah was ten times worse. Jackson sent Chase a text, then put his cell in his pocket.

His thoughts returned to Freezergate and the heated argument he'd had with his sister that morning. He'd made the mistake of telling Mariah he was romantically interested in Grace, and she'd erupted like Mount St. Helens. She'd threatened to disown him if he hooked up with the competition again, and insisted they summon Chase home for an emergency family meeting.

A week later, Mariah was still giving him the cold shoulder, and the tension inside Lillian's was stifling his creativity. He had a week to make three speciality cakes, but hadn't started them yet. Jackson couldn't get Mariah's accusations out of his mind, and when he wasn't reliving their argument he was fantasizing about Grace. Daydreaming about her mouth, her fine feminine shape, squeezing her plump, juicy ass. Tomorrow, after basketball practice, he was going to Lillian's and he wasn't leaving until he finished the wedding cakes he'd been commissioned to make.

"Are you inviting Grace to the Heritage Arts and Awards dinner?"

"So Mariah can kill me with her bare hands? No way. I'm flying solo that night." To please Diego's wife, Ana Sofia, he'd bought two tickets to the black-tie event, but he didn't know which of his female friends to invite. *Damn, I wish I could take Grace*, he thought. He enjoyed her company, knew she'd look great on his arm, but if they went to the awards dinner together the whole world would know they were an item, and Mariah would be pissed if she found out he was romancing the enemy.

Jackson remembered the conversation he'd had with his sister two days earlier in the bakery storage room and felt guilty, knew he'd done wrong. While doing inventory Mariah had asked him point-blank if he was sleeping with Grace, and he'd told her there was nothing gone on. Sweating profusely, he'd swiftly changed the subject, got his sister talking about the new recipes she was working on for the Bite of Seattle festival and fled the room the moment Kelsey walked in, looking for a rolling pin.

"Give it up to the Ballet Misfits for their 220-170 win! Better luck next time, Curvy Crashers," the announcer said. "And a special thank-you to all the fans who braved the rain to come out and cheer on the home team."

While the crowd filed out of the stadium, Jackson and Diego finished their beers.

"I'll be right back. I want to see Grace before she leaves."

Diego glanced at his watch. "If you're not back in ten minutes, I'm out of here."

"What's the rush? It's only five o'clock and the boxing match won't start for hours."

"Yeah, but if we turn up late the food will be gone and I'm starving."

Jackson left the stands and walked through the tunnel, searching for Grace. He stood in the hallway, waiting patiently as players streamed out of the locker rooms, but he didn't see number forty-nine. An Asian woman with dyed red hair and heavy makeup flashed him a salacious smile and he nodded in greeting. "Do you know Grace Nicholas?" he asked, taking his cell out of his pocket to check for missed calls. "Is she still in the changing room?"

"Yeah, the trainer's looking at her knee. She banged it up pretty bad in the second period, but Shannon's taking good care of her."

Jackson took off down the hall, pushed open the door marked Home Team and strode inside. He smelled soap and perfume, noticed the Nike posters on the walls featuring famous female athletes and heard the distant sound of voices.

Entering the showers, he saw Grace and stopped dead in his tracks. She was sitting on a wooden bench, wearing nothing but a black sports bra and boy shorts, clutching her right knee.

"Grace, baby, are you okay?"

Surprise colored her cheeks. "Jackson, what are you doing here?"

"I came to cheer on the home team, of course. You were amazing out there."

"But the game wasn't even close. We lost by fifty points," she argued.

"So? I think you were spectacular tonight, and that's all that matters."

"Sir, you have to leave. Fans aren't allowed in the changing rooms."

"I'm Grace's boyfriend. Who are you?"

"The trainer for the Curvy Crashers," he replied, standing to his full height.

Jackson blinked, regarded the heavyset man in the weathered Reebok sweatsuit that had his name stitched on the top left and swallowed a laugh. He couldn't believe this big, burly giant with the piercings and tattoos had a female name. "Bro, I got it from here. I'll take care of my girl."

The trainer's face fell and he glanced at Grace with a pleading look. "I'll take you home."

"Shannon, I'm fine. Really. It's a small bruise. No biggie."

"Are you sure?" he questioned, a frown wedged between his thick, fuzzy unibrow. "The last time you told me you were fine you ended up in the emergency room in excruciating pain."

"That's not going to happen on my watch." Jackson stalked over to the bench, sat down and inspected Grace's knee. It was bruised, but she stood without difficulty and gave the sour-faced trainer a hug. "I'll see you at practice next week."

Shannon shuffled out of the room with his head down and his shoulders bent.

"I wasn't expecting to see you tonight."

Jackson was trying to concentrate, but it was hard to focus when Grace was standing in front of him practically naked. God had blessed her in many ways and he admired them all. The large breasts, the flat stomach, thick thighs and long, toned legs. His eyes zeroed in on her silver belly ring and Jackson smiled to himself. What else was she hiding? Did she have another piercing down south? Swallowing hard, he pictured them at his house, doing wicked and salacious things in his bedroom, things that would make a rock star blush—

"Earth to Jackson."

At the sound of her voice, he blinked and shook the thought from his mind, giving Grace his full attention. "Why didn't you remind me about your game tonight?"

"Because you think roller derby is a joke and I didn't want you making fun of me."

"I'd never do that. You're strong and powerful and I don't want you to kick my ass!"

"Damn right, and don't you forget it."

Jackson grabbed her around the waist and pulled her down onto his lap. To make her laugh, he screwed his eyes shut and waved a hand in front of his nose. "You stink!"

"Thanks a lot." Grace stuck out her tongue and gave him a shot on the arm. "You sure know how to make a girl feel good after a heartbreaking loss."

"Just doing my part, bae."

Grace linked her hands around his neck and snuggled against him, and Jackson decided there was nothing better than holding her in his arms. "Is forty-nine your favorite number?"

She dropped her gaze to her lap, blew out a deep breath and shook her head.

"What is it?"

"My mom was forty-nine years old when she died." Tears filled her voice, swam in her eyes, and she swallowed hard. "I wear the number in remembrance of her."

They sat in silence, didn't speak, just held each other tight.

"Your mom is gone, but she's in your heart forever so don't run from your memories of her, embrace them," Jackson said in a soothing tone. "I was incredibly close to my grandfather, Oscar, and when he died it felt like my heart had been ripped out of my chest..."

Jackson trailed off, taking a moment to gather his thoughts. He hadn't planned to tell Grace about his grandfather's death, but he felt compelled to, hoped his words gave her strength.

"You know what helped me heal?"

Grace sniffed, shook her head. "No. What?"

"Doing all the things we loved doing together."

"Was your grandfather an avid sportsman, too?"

"Yes. I learned everything I know about golf—*and* women—from him."

"That explains why you have so many female admirers."

"Does that bother you?" he asked, studying her face for clues. Grace wasn't the jealous type, didn't give off that vibe, but Jackson wanted to know for sure. He didn't want to upset her and wanted to be upfront about everything. "Would you prefer if I didn't hang out with my exes?"

"No, of course not. You can do what you want. I have no claims to you."

Ouch. Her words were a slap in the face and moments passed before he recovered.

"It doesn't matter what I think. You told Shannon I'm your girlfriend so he wouldn't kick you out of here, but I'm not."

"Do you want to be?"

"So you can break my heart?" she quipped, shaking her head. "No, thanks. I'll pass."

"Grace, you act like you're the only one who's been hurt. I've been lied to, cheated on and betrayed."

"You have? No way. Someone actually cheated on you?"

"Why does that surprise you?"

"Because you're attractive and successful and smart," she said. "You can have any woman you want, and you probably have!"

"Not any woman. I don't have you."

A seductive grin curled her lips. "Do you want me?"

"Baby, you have no idea."

"Then what are you waiting for?" she teased, cocking her head. "Let's do this."

Her words excited him, caused his erection to harden and strain against his boxer shorts. Jackson kissed her with a savage intensity, mated hungrily with her tongue as it danced around his mouth. He'd never done anything like this before, never had sex in a women's locker room, but everything about it turned him on. The spontaneity. The excitement. The thrill of getting caught in the act—again.

Grace unbuttoned his shirt, shrugged it down his shoulders then tossed it to the floor as if it was a filthy rag rather than a Kenneth Cole design. Rocking her hips against his crotch, she kissed from his earlobe to his neck and along his shoulders. Grace turned him out with her tongue, licked and sucked his nipples as if she was starving and he was the main course.

Kicking off his shoes, he tightened his hold on her hips and stood to his feet.

"Jackson, what are you doing?" Grace tossed her head back and shrieked with laughter. "If you throw out your back and end up on bed rest, don't blame me."

"As long as you're my sexy nurse, it's all good."

"Where are we going?" she asked, her words a breathless pant.

"To get you clean, of course. You're dirty, remember?"

Realization dawned and her face lit up. "You're a *very* bad boy, Jackson Drayson."

"I know, and you love it."

"You're right, baby, I do." Grace clamped her thighs around his waist and placed kisses along his ear and neck. "Being with you makes me high, gives me a rush…"

Jackson entered the shower stall farthest from the locker room, stripped off the rest of his clothes and turned the water on full blast. Steam rose, filling the air, but there was no mistaking her excitement. It shone in her eyes, covered her face, tickled her lips. "Take off your panties, or I'll rip them off," he commanded, setting her down on the ground.

"I like how you think."

"And I like that ass, so turn around, bend over and touch those pretty pink toes."

Chapter 9

Instantly wet, her body throbbing with need, Grace licked her lips as her eyes slid down Jackson's naked body. Lean and toned, he had the physique of a man who spent hours lifting weights at the gym, and staring at his erection made her mouth dry. Thinking about making love to him, of finally doing all the wicked things she'd fantasized about in her dreams, left her breathless and panting for the main event.

"I need you," he declared, his tone a husky growl. "Right here, right now…"

Hypnotized by his touch and his assertive, take-charge tone, Grace did as she was told, assuming the position he'd demanded. His mouth, tongue and hands paid homage to her curves, and her body trembled as he placed kisses down her spine.

"I'm desperate for you, Grace. Have been since the first time you entered Lillian's."

"Then what took you so long to make your move?"

"I don't want a girlfriend, just sex, and I didn't want to give you the wrong impression."

"I don't want anything long-term, either."

"I'm glad we're on the same page."

Jackson kissed her and she laughed inside his mouth. He brushed his nose against hers, told her she was sexy, captivating, said she belonged to him and no one else. Taking her bottom lip between his teeth, he ran his hands up her thighs to her sex. He swirled his fingers in her dark, tight curls, played with them, tugged on them.

Massaging her outer lips with slow, sensual strokes made her thighs quiver. Jackson mashed her breasts together and sucked her erect nipples into his mouth, sucking so vigorously that pleasure and pain exploded inside her body in equal measures.

"Grace, is this what you want? Is this how you like it?"

"Oh, yes," she moaned. "Deeper, Jackson, harder, faster…"

His fingers worked their magic between her legs, stirring and probing her wet clit. Her breathing grew thicker, louder, and when Jackson rubbed his erection against her ass Grace cried out. The move triggered an orgasm so powerful her knees gave out and she collapsed against him. Skin-to-skin, her back pressed flat against his chest, water raining down on them from the showerhead, Grace decided it was the sexiest, most erotic moment of her life. And she wanted more. Jackson must have read her thoughts, sensed what she was thinking, because he slid his hand from between her legs, stalked over to their clothes scattered around the room and took a condom out of his jeans. He ripped open the gold packet and rolled the condom down his shaft.

Excitement fluttered inside Grace's belly. The water was warm and nice, felt good against her skin. Approaching her with a broad grin, his body glistening with water, Jackson looked more like an underwear model than a baker, but when Grace shared her thoughts he laughed. "Tonight, I'll be anything you want me to be."

"I bet you say that to *all* of your customers," she joked with a teasing smile.

"No, just you. You're one in a million, Grace, and I'm going to prove it right now."

Spreading her legs wide, she braced her hands against the wall and arched her back. Slowly, he eased the tip of his erection inside her sex, taking his time filling her with his impressive length. Savoring the moment and how amazing Jackson felt inside her, she pressed her eyes shut and threw her head back. His erection was the best thing that had ever happened to her. It was an instrument of pleasure, and her body responded eagerly to his slow, penetrating stroke.

Taking his hands in hers, Grace used them to roughly cup her breasts. He tweaked her nipples, plucked them, rolled them between his fingers, sending her body into an erotic tailspin. Jackson pumped his hips, thrust powerfully inside her, used his erection to turn her out. Her ears tingled, her knees buckled and her toes curled.

Grabbing a fistful of her hair, he pulled her face toward his and kissed her hard on the mouth. The heat from his tongue spread through her body, setting it on fire. Grace was losing it, didn't know how much more she could take. Jackson moved faster, thrusting,

"FAST FIVE" READER SURVEY

Your participation entitles you to:
✳ 4 Thank-You Gifts Worth Over $20!

Complete the survey in minutes.

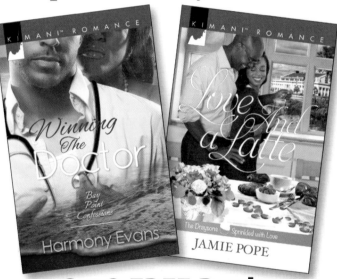

Get **2 FREE** Books

See inside for details.

Dear Reader,

Since you are a lover of our books, your opinions are important to us... and so is your time.

That's why we made sure your **"FAST FIVE" READER SURVEY** can be completed in just a few minutes. Your answers to the five questions will help us remain at the forefront of women's fiction.

And, as a thank-you for participating, we'd like to send you **4 FREE THANK-YOU GIFTS!**

Enjoy your gifts with our appreciation,

Pam Powers

To get your
4 FREE THANK-YOU GIFTS:

✴ Quickly complete the "Fast Five" Reader Survey and return the insert.

"FAST FIVE" READER SURVEY

1	Do you sometimes read a book a second or third time?	○ Yes ○ No
2	Do you often choose reading over other forms of entertainment such as television?	○ Yes ○ No
3	When you were a child, did someone regularly read aloud to you?	○ Yes ○ No
4	Do you sometimes take a book with you when you travel outside the home?	○ Yes ○ No
5	In addition to books, do you regularly read newspapers and magazines?	○ Yes ○ No

YES! I have completed the above Reader Survey. Please send me my 4 FREE GIFTS (gifts worth over $20 retail). I understand that I am under no obligation to buy anything, as explained on the back of this card.

168/368 XDL GJ5L

FIRST NAME

LAST NAME

ADDRESS

APT.#

CITY

STATE/PROV.

ZIP/POSTAL CODE

K-816-SFF15

READER SERVICE—Here's how it works:

BUSINESS REPLY MAIL
FIRST-CLASS MAIL   PERMIT NO. 717   BUFFALO, NY

POSTAGE WILL BE PAID BY ADDRESSEE

READER SERVICE
PO BOX 1867
BUFFALO NY 14240-9952

NO POSTAGE
NECESSARY
IF MAILED
IN THE
UNITED STATES

▼ If offer card is missing write to: Reader Service, P.O. Box 1867, Buffalo, NY 14240-1867 or visit www.ReaderService.com ▼

pumping, pounding into her with all his might. Their lovemaking was savage and intense, everything Grace wanted and more.

"Baby, come," he urged, reverently massaging her backside. "Come for me again, and this time don't hold back. Explode for me, baby. Do it now."

Arching her back, she opened her eyes and shot him a sultry smile. "You first."

Jackson spanked her, slapping her bottom once, twice, three spine-tingling times. Grace moaned, then begged him to do it again.

"Keep talking like that and I'll keep you in this shower for the rest of the night," he vowed, slowly licking his lips. "Is that what you want?"

Yes! Yes! Yes! she thought, poking out her butt and rocking against his groin.

"You're a hellcat, and I love it."

Grace raised an eyebrow, feigned an innocent look. "Is that all you love?"

"No. I love your intelligence, and wit, and how you walk into a room and command everyone's attention, and this, of course…" Jackson slid his hands between her legs. "I think I love this the most. It's mine now. Understood?"

His words and his powerful thrusts caused dynamite to explode inside her body. His erection swelled, filling her, consuming her sex. Cursing, he gripped her shoulders, increased his pace, moving faster, thrusting deeper still. The water drowned out his guttural groans as he climaxed, and Grace's frenzied, out-of-control screams. Savoring the feel of him, the sound of his voice, his slow, passionate kisses, she collapsed against the shower wall, trying to catch her breath.

"The next time I come in here I'll have to remember to lock the door."

"Don't bother," he said with an impish grin. "I'll break it down to get to you."

Grace stepped past him. Her legs were wobbly, but she had to get dressed. She searched the floor for her panties. "We better get out of here before the cleaning crew arrives."

"Where do you think you're going?" Jackson captured her around the waist, pulled her back into the shower stall and drew the curtain. "Not so fast, Ms. Nicholas. We're not done yet."

Her eyes widened. "We're not?"

"No. Not until you come inside my mouth." Without warning, Jackson dropped to his knees, hiked her leg up in the air and dipped his tongue inside her, swirling it around in slow, sensual circles, using it as a weapon. He did things with his lips and teeth she'd never experienced, but she enjoyed every second. His mouth hit her pleasure zone over and over again, holding her in place as she unraveled, coming undone.

Hot and tingly all over, she pumped her hips, increasing her pace, desperately chasing her third orgasm. Then it hit, and once the tremors in her sex started she couldn't stop them.

Grace turned into the cul-de-sac, noticed all the lights were on in the house and slammed on her brakes. Through the living room curtains, she spotted someone pacing swiftly back and forth, with their hands propped on their hips, and she frowned. What the hell? The figure could only be one person: her dad. Why wasn't he in bed? Had he had another nightmare? Is that why he was up? He'd called her numerous times that evening, but since he didn't leave a message she didn't phone back and figured she'd talk to him tomorrow instead.

Besides, she'd been tied up—literally—and Jackson wouldn't let her leave his house until she'd had something to eat. After their tryst in the woman's locker room, Jackson had insisted they have a romantic dinner at a trendy, downtown restaurant followed by a nightcap at his place. Promising her an orgasm she'd never forget, he'd bound her hands together with a Burberry scarf, then proceeded to lick her from head to toe, as if she was a Popsicle. An orgasm had rocked her body, leaving her spent and weak, and by the time Jackson slid his erection inside her she was a trembling, quivering mess. They'd enjoyed an explosive night of sex, had made love so many times, Grace was sore all over, but she'd hook up with Jackson again in a heartbeat. The man had a way with words—and had scrumptious lips—and she was counting down until their next date. He was taking her to the symphony tomorrow, then for Creole food, and Grace was so anxious to see him again he was all she could think about.

Sensing what was about to happen next, Grace parked under a lamppost, took her cell phone out of the cup holder and punched in Bronwyn's number. No answer. Determined to speak to her friend, Grace hung up and hit Redial. On the third try, a female voice grunted, "Hello?" and she sighed in relief.

"Bronwyn, I need a favor."

"Grace? Is everything okay?"

"Of course. Everything's great."

"Are you sure? It's…" Bronwyn trailed off speaking,

then gasped. "It's three o'clock in the morning. Where are you? What's going on?"

"Sorry for waking you up, but I need a favor," Grace repeated, her eyes glued to her childhood home. Her father was still pacing, but now he was clutching the cordless phone in his hands, and Grace feared he was calling their friends and family to find out where she was.

"Sure, girl, anything for you. What's up?"

"If my dad calls and asks where I've been, tell him I was with you."

"What's going on? Why are you lying to your old man? Who are you with?"

"I'll explain tomorrow. Just cover for me, okay?"

Bronwyn squealed and Grace feared she'd go deaf in her right ear.

"It's that hottie baker from Lillian's, isn't it? I knew you liked him!"

"Bronwyn, focus—"

"Of course, I'll cover for you. We're girls and, since I love gossip almost as much as I love your macaroon bites, you can tell me about your date with the dreamy baker when I return from my business trip next week. You're making brunch on Wednesday. Don't forget!"

Grace laughed, unable to believe her best friend was hitting her up for a home-cooked meal during her time of need. Desperate, she agreed, but groaned inwardly when Bronwyn squealed again.

"I'm off, so we can spend the whole day together." She added, in a cheeky voice, "That's unless you're not *doing*, I mean, seeing the hottie baker. *Ciao, mamacita!*"

Ending the call, she opened the garage with a click of a button and drove inside. Like a ghost, her dad appeared in the doorway. Annoyed, Grace expelled a deep breath and stepped out of the car. Forcing a smile, she tried to be as casual as possible. "Hey, Dad. You're up late—"

"You missed dinner."

Guilt troubled her conscience, but Grace pushed aside the feeling, telling herself she'd done nothing wrong. She'd spent the night with an exciting, exhilarating man who loved her like she'd never been loved before, and just the thought of him—and his dynamic moves between the sheets—made her body yearn for more. "I had other plans." Grace strode inside and felt a pang of sadness, an overwhelming sense of loss. Her mom would never welcome her home with a hug and kiss again, and the bitter realization brought tears to her eyes. "Dad, it's been a long day. I'm going to bed. We'll talk in the morning, okay?"

"No, we'll talk now." He stood in front of the staircase, cutting off her escape route. "Ainsworth and his parents wanted to meet you, but you were a no-show."

Grace winced. Feeling guilty for letting him down, she couldn't look him in the eye for fear he'd know the truth. "Dad, I'm sorry. It completely slipped my mind."

"I figured as much, so I called to remind you. Why didn't you answer your phone?"

Because I was with Jackson, and nothing else mattered.

"Ainsworth was very disappointed, so I suggested he come by the shop on Friday." His face brightened and his tone softened. "You'll be in, right, pumpkin?"

"Yes, of course, but I have tons of work to do."

"Please? For me? If sales continue to decline at the bakery we're going to need more investors, and if you and Ainsworth become a couple, his parents will definitely back the shop."

"Fine, I'll have a drink with him." Grace raised an index finger. "One coffee. That's it."

"One last thing. We're having dinner at the Ventura estate next Sunday so don't make any other plans. This is important."

"Good night, Dad. I'll see you in the morning."

He leaned in and kissed her forehead. "Have you been drinking?"

Grace swallowed hard, racking her brain for a suitable explanation.

Sniffing the air, he scrutinized her face. "Yes, you definitely smell of alcohol. What's going on? You don't drink and drive. Your mother and I raised you better than that."

"I haven't been drinking, per se. I had a whiskey pear tart for dessert."

Nodding in understanding, he patted her forearm good-naturedly. "Was it good?"

"The best I've ever had."

Grace kissed her dad on the cheek and headed downstairs. Thoughts of Jackson on her mind, she strode into her bedroom suite with a smile on her face and a song in her heart, and the hottie baker was the reason why.

Chapter 10

Grace slipped on her Prada sunglasses, threw open the French doors and strode along the stone walkway, feeling like a million bucks. Clad in a polka-dot bikini, her arms filled with magazines, she set off for the pool, wanting to take advantage of the hot July weather.

Plopping down onto an orange lounge chair, Grace closed her eyes and soaked in the world around her. She heard birds chirping, felt the sun on her face and decided it was going to be a great day. Better than yesterday.

Her body tensed. Yesterday had been a disaster at the shop. Two baristas had called in sick, another had burned her arm on the stove, which resulted in a trip to the emergency room, and a cashier had accidently knocked over a German chocolate cake. Grace shuddered at the memory of the exchange she'd had with the

customer who'd arrived to pick up the ruined gradua-
tion cake and hoped she never saw the foul-mouthed
attorney again.

All week, she'd been working around the clock—
manning the till because the bakery was short-staffed,
interviewing potential candidates for the head baker
position, cleaning the shop after closing—so when her
dad suggested she take today off, she'd accepted his
offer without hesitation. Rashad J was playing on her
cell phone, singing about lost love, and the sound of his
soothing, soulful voice put Grace in a tranquil mood.

Grace heard her cell buzz, knew she had a new text
message and grabbed her phone off the side table. She
hoped it wasn't Ainsworth. They'd met at the shop last
week and he'd been blowing up her phone ever since.
He'd invited her to the Seattle Art Walk, and although
Grace had no plans for Sunday she'd politely declined
his offer. Ainsworth was a conservative man, with old-
fashioned family values, a catch according to her father.
He was nice, sure, chivalrous, too, but Grace wasn't
attracted to him. The Ventura family had money like
Oprah, but Ainsworth didn't do it for her. Didn't ex-
cite her. Not the way Jackson did. Jackson showered
her with affection, knew how to make her laugh and,
most important, treated her like his equal, not a weak,
docile woman who needed his protection. Ainsworth
wanted a puppet, a Stepford wife, and if not for her father she'd have nothing to do with him.

Noting the time, she realized she'd forgotten to have
lunch and decided to order in. Surprised, but pleased to
see the message was from Jackson, Grace bolted upright
in her chair. They'd been texting each other all morning, and every time his name popped up in her inbox

her heart soared. Smiling from ear to ear, she slowly and carefully read his latest message.

Do you want some company? I'll bring you lunch and a kiss.

At the thought of seeing Jackson again, desire warmed her skin and images of last night flashed in her mind. Salsa dancing at the Corbu Lounge. Feeding each other appetizers in their cozy booth. The French kiss that led to a quickie in the darkened coatroom. Locking them inside, he'd yanked down her panties, slipped on a condom and taken her from behind. His behavior had been shocking and unexpected, but Grace didn't stop him. She'd been aroused, turned on by his raunchy sex talk, and encouraged his advances. Minutes later, she'd experienced an orgasm so explosive she'd cursed in Spanish. The memory of their lovemaking made Grace yearn for more. Her gaze strayed to the pool, zeroed in on the cobalt-blue water, and suddenly, sexing Jackson was all she could think about.

Grace considered her response, weighing the pros and cons of inviting Jackson over. Her dad was at work, the housekeeper would be finished and leaving within the hour and Grace would have the entire house to herself. She wanted to see Jackson, but knew if he came over they'd end up in bed, and if her dad found out, he'd never forgive her for disrespecting his home.

Absorbed in composing her message, she didn't notice Edwina was standing in front of her lounge chair until the housekeeper cleared her throat.

"I brought you a snack," she said, resting a tray filled

with fruits and vegetables on the side table. "Can I get you anything else before I leave?"

"No, thank you, Edwina. That will be all. Have fun with your grandkids this afternoon."

"I will, Ms. Grace. See you on Monday."

Settling back in her seat, she crossed her legs at the ankles. Grace enjoyed texting Jackson and cracked up at his jokes. She ate up his compliments like Rocky Road ice cream and couldn't get enough of his wit and humor. Add to that, he was an exquisite lover. It was no surprise she was hot for him. Jackson was a great guy, exactly what she needed in her life, and Grace considered herself lucky to be dating one of the sexiest bachelors in the city. It could all be over tomorrow, and she was going to have fun while it lasted.

"Honey, I'm home!"

Hearing her best friend's voice, Grace tore her gaze away from her cell and glanced at the wooden gate. Looking fresh and vibrant in her sleeveless pink romper, Bronwyn breezed through the backyard, smiling and waving frantically, as if they hadn't seen each other in months rather than a few days.

"Hey, girl, how are you doing?"

Bronwyn groaned and clutched her stomach. "I'm starving, so please feed me!"

"Help yourself." Grace gestured to the table. "Eat as much as you'd like."

Dropping onto a lounge chair, she wrinkled her nose and puckered her lips. "I can't eat this. I need *real* food. Like one of your amazing sriracha burgers with sweet potato fries, and pecan pie for dessert."

"Not today. I don't feel like cooking. Maybe another time."

"Grace, you've been saying that for over a year. When are you going to return to the kitchen and start cooking again? Your customers are dying to know, and so am I."

"I don't want to argue, Bronwyn, so drop it."

"I can't. This pity party has lasted long enough."

Pity party? Pain stabbed her heart. *I lost my mom, not my favorite pair of earrings.*

"I know the last year has been rough on you, but you're a fighter..."

Too choked up to speak, water filling her eyes, Grace dropped her gaze to her lap.

"You *can* overcome this, so dust your apron off and get back in the kitchen."

Her nose itched and her vision blurred but she didn't break down. Was Bronwyn right? Should she quit working in the office and resume baking? Was that the answer to her problems?

"My bridal shower is three weeks away and I need you to whip up some of your scrumptious pastries for the party," she said with a pleading expression on her face. "I want Rodolfo's bitchy mother to like me and your confections are my secret weapon. One bite of your mango cheesecake and the old biddy will be eating out of the palm of my hand, *literally*!"

A giggle fell from Grace's mouth. Leave it to Bronwyn to make her laugh.

"I want to hear what happened with you and baker boy while I was away, so dish the dirt."

"What dirt?" she asked, playing coy. "We've hooked up a few times. No biggie."

Bronwyn tucked her feet under her bottom. "I want

to know everything. Where was your first time? Is Jackson a good lover? Does he go down south?"

Does. He. Ever. Grace couldn't put her thoughts into words, didn't even try. Her friend wouldn't understand, and she didn't want Bronwyn to tease her for gushing about Jackson. "He's incredible," she said quietly, a grin tugging at her mouth. "Let's just leave it at that."

Bronwyn whistled. "I believe you. Your smile is so wide it's blinding!"

To prevent herself from blurting out the truth, Grace popped a piece of watermelon into her mouth. She loved Bronwyn and hated keeping secrets from her, but she didn't feel comfortable discussing her sex life with her best friend. Jackson was special to her, important, and she didn't want to taint their relationship by revealing intimate details about him. It had been a month since Freezergate, but they'd spent so much time together it felt like years had passed since their infamous date at Lillian's, and Grace didn't want to betray his trust.

"What are you doing tonight?"

Jackson, she thought, hiding a smirk.

"Rodolfo's hanging out with his brothers, so I thought we could have a girl's night in."

"Sorry, but I have plans with Jackson. He's taking me to Little India for dinner."

"Great restaurant," Bronwyn said, vigorously nodding. "But can he afford it?"

"What's that supposed to mean?"

"He's not exactly rolling in dough and the entrees start at a hundred bucks."

"Of course he can," she snapped, struggling to control her temper. "He's not a gold digger, if that's what you're implying. Jackson's got plenty of money and he doesn't need mine."

"Jackson's hot, and I'm sure he's fantastic in bed, but don't fall for him. He's a player, just like Phillip, and he'll never, ever commit to you."

Grace wore a composed expression on her face, didn't argue, but inside she was seething. Bronwyn didn't know Jackson, and had no right to badmouth him.

"Things started off great with Philip, too, but we both know how that turned out," Bronwyn continued, her tone matter-of-fact. "Three months into your relationship he was hitting you up for money, demanding expensive gifts and using your Jag to pick up other women."

"Jackson's different. He's nothing like Phillip."

"I hope so, because I don't want to see you get hurt again."

Me, too, Grace thought, hanging her head. *I don't think my heart could take it.*

"Guys like Jackson don't change—"

"We're not serious, so you have nothing to worry about," she said with a shrug. "Except Rodolfo's bitchy mother ruining your big day!"

Bronwyn laughed and the sound of her high-pitched giggles made Grace smile.

"What are you wearing for your date?"

"I don't know. I haven't decided yet. Why?"

"Just make sure it's fabulous. Little India is the hottest new restaurant in town so you have to look amazing tonight." Bronwyn got up from the lounge chair and dragged Grace to her feet. "Let's head inside. I'll make lunch, then I'll help you get ready for your date."

Grace groaned. "Do I have a choice?"

"No, heifer, you don't. Time to go. Beauty waits for no one!"

Grace stood in front of the full-length bedroom mirror, her gaze narrowed, assessing her appearance. The sultry makeup, the peacock-blue dress, the gladiator sandals that drew attention to her long legs. Deciding her outfit was a winner, Grace smiled at her reflection, marveling at how sophisticated she looked in her designer ensemble.

Opening her jewelry box, she found her diamond hoop earrings. After Bronwyn left she'd taken a long, luxurious bubble bath, but as Grace entered her walk-in closet she heard her mother's voice in her ears and ditched the outfit Bronwyn had selected for her to wear.

"Always dress like you're going to meet your worst enemy," Rosemary had advised her numerous times. "And wear red lipstick. Men will find you irresistible."

With that thought in mind, she'd curled her hair and applied her favorite lipstick. The moment Grace put on the metallic sheath dress and peep-toe sandals she knew Jackson wouldn't be able to keep his hands off her. She wanted to impress him and couldn't wait to see the look on his face when she walked into Little India in her sexy outfit.

The home phone rang, interrupting her thoughts, and an unknown number appeared on the screen. "Hello?" she asked, hoping it wasn't a telemarketer.

"Grace, it's me. Don't hang up!"

Disgust curled her lips and seeped into her tone. "What do you want?"

"To see you. To apologize for ruining what we had."

"Phillip, I have nothing to say to you, so please leave me alone."

"I can't. We had something special once and I want you back."

His loud, strident voice pierced her eardrum, grating on her nerves. Why did Phillip have to be obnoxious? Why couldn't he respect her wishes and back off? When was he going to get it through his head they were over for good? Desperate to end their conversation, she said, "Save your breath because there's nothing you can say or do to change my mind. Bye."

"Baby, don't do this to me. We're magic together and I need you in my life."

"You should have thought of that before you deceived me."

"Hear me out," he said, sounding as cocky as ever, as if he was the one calling the shots. "I messed up. I admit it. Please find it in your heart to forgive me…"

Grace couldn't. Didn't have it in her. Phillip didn't deserve her and furthermore she had her eye on someone else—a hottie baker with a heart of gold. Grace couldn't go five minutes without thinking about Jackson and wanted to spend all of her free time with him. She was scared of being hurt again, but her heart was leading her straight to her biggest competitor.

"The Heritage Arts and Awards dinner is on Saturday and I want you to be my date."

"Why? So I can pay your way? No, thanks. I'm through being your meal ticket."

"Baby, let's talk about this. I miss you and I know you miss me."

Grace scoffed. "Yeah, about as much as I miss having pneumonia!"

"This is silly. I'm coming over. I need to see you. We have to talk face-to-face."

"Suit yourself, but I won't be here. I have a date."

"A—a date!" he stammered, his voice a pitiful squeak. "With who—"

"A *real* man who knows how to treat a woman." *And how to make my body sing*, she added silently, swiping her satin clutch off the dresser and tucking it under her arm. Men like Phillip—cocky, slick-talking types— were as common as flour in a bakery, but Jackson was one of a kind, and Grace wanted to be with him, not arguing with her ex on the phone.

"I don't want you dating other guys—"

"I don't care what you want," Grace snapped, wishing she could reach through the phone and whack him with her purse. "We're through, and so is this conversation. See ya!"

Grace dropped the cordless on the cradle and sailed through her bedroom door, thinking about her conversation with Phillip. He'd given her an idea. The Heritage Arts and Awards dinner recognized outstanding educators, artists and cultural leaders for their significant contributions to society, and she wanted to attend the black-tie event.

Fond memories flooded her mind. Three years earlier, she'd attended the awards show with her mother and they'd had the time of their lives. Drinking champagne. Dancing to old-school classics. Mingling with the beautiful people, handing out hugs and business cards. Her mother was gone, but she wanted to attend the event in Rosemary's honor. And she wanted Jackson to be her date. Grace was scared of going public with their relationship, knew her dad would be livid when he discovered she was dating the competition, but she adored Jackson and wanted the world to know they were a couple—especially his ex-girlfriends and female admirers.

Her cell phone buzzed and Grace fished it out of her purse. Reading Jackson's text message, she felt her heart skip a beat and a smile overwhelm her mouth.

Change of plans, beautiful. Meet me at home.

Anything for you, she thought, sailing through her bedroom door. Grace had never felt his good, this sexy and desirable, and Jackson was the reason why. He was always touching her, kissing her, telling her how beautiful and smart she was, and his words bolstered her confidence.

Grace unlocked her car, slid inside the driver's seat and started the engine. Minutes later, she was cruising down the street, singing along with the Sade song playing on the radio.

As she drove, a warm breeze flowed through the sunroof and her thoughts turned to Jackson. The more time they spent together, the more Grace desired him, wished he was her boyfriend and not just her lover. Isn't that why she was going to invite Jackson to the awards dinner? Because she wanted the whole world to know he was hers, and she was his? Initially, they'd only been interested in a sexual relationship, but deep down Grace wanted more, and hoped Jackson did, too.

Anxious to see him, Grace stepped on the gas and weaved in and out of traffic, driving with more finesse than a race car driver. Her speed climbed, and so did her pulse, thundering loudly in her ears. Grace hoped

Jackson had condoms at home because she wanted to make love, and a quickie before dinner was the perfect way to start the night.

Chapter 11

"Perfect timing. I just got back from the grocery store," Jackson said from the doorway of his house, his expression warm and welcoming, a broad grin on his lips. "Now we have everything we need to make a delicious meal *and* rum truffles!"

"I thought we were going to Little India for dinner."

"Why, when we can cook from the comfort of home?"

Hiding a grin, Grace stuck out her tongue. "Cheapskate!"

Chuckling, Jackson pulled her into his open arms. "Baby, I want you all to myself tonight. I don't want to share you with anyone else, or compete for your attention."

His words, and his touch along her hips, made her heart soar like the birds in the sky.

"I missed you," he said, his husky voice thick with desire. "Come here."

Jackson kissed her, slowly, thoughtfully, as if he was savoring the taste of her mouth. His kiss excited her and his cologne aroused her senses, stirring powerful emotions inside her. Lust consumed her, making it impossible for Grace to control her sexual desires. She moaned into his mouth, linked her arms around his neck, loving his closeness.

He slipped his tongue into her mouth, hungrily mated with hers, devouring her. Moving closer, Grace playfully nibbled at the corners of his mouth, teasing and licking it. They were a perfect fit, an ideal match, and she relished being in his arms. In the bedroom, Jackson satisfied her every wish, and Grace was desperate for him, eager to feel him inside her one more time. Every night, after making love, they'd cuddle in bed, talking for hours, and those memories would stay with her forever.

"We better stop," he said between kisses, nuzzling his nose against hers. "I have onions sautéing on the stove and I don't want to burn the house down."

At the thought of their disastrous first date, Grace laughed out loud. "You're never going to let me live that down, are you?"

"Nope. Never!" Resting his hands on her hips, he steered her down the hallway and through the main floor. She loved the feel of Jackson's place, how spacious, bright and comfortable it was. Every time Grace looked at the mosaic paintings, handmade sculptures and dark wood carvings, she felt as if she'd stepped into a museum. His bachelor pad was filled with leather couches, low-hanging lights, silken drapes and every electronic device known to man. Grace noted how clean the living room was, how the floors and tables gleamed and sparkled, and suspected he had a female house-keeper.

Entering the kitchen, Grace inhaled the piquant aroma in the air. Hip-hop music was playing on the stereo system and the infectious beat of the song made Grace feel like dancing around the room. Mixing bowls filled with vegetables, packaged meat and expensive wine bottles sat on the countertop. "What are you making?"

"Not me, *we*," he amended, affectionately patting her hips. "We're making lentil soup, Tandoori chicken salad, lamb shakuti and coconut rice."

Laughing off his comment, she leaned into him, enjoying the warmth of his touch. "And for dessert?"

"Each other."

Another passionate kiss and her thoughts spun out of control. *I could definitely get used to this*, she decided, circling her arms around his waist. *I could stay here with Jackson forever.*

"I have something for you." Jackson strode into the pantry and flipped on the light.

Sliding onto one of the stools at the breakfast bar, Grace picked up the bottle of chili sauce and scanned the ingredients. Since meeting Jackson, she'd been eating out of control, and if she didn't cut back on the sweets she wouldn't be able to fit into her bridesmaid dress for Bronwyn's wedding, and her best friend would kill her for gaining weight.

"What do you think? Hilarious, right?"

Grace looked up, saw the apron Jackson was holding and burst out laughing, giggling until tears filled her eyes. It was fuchsia, covered in butcher knives, and the caption under the pocket read, I'm the Chef. If You

Don't Follow My Instructions, I'll Stab You! Moved by his thoughtfulness Grace beamed. "You know me so well. I love it."

Jackson smiled wider than a kid perched on Santa's lap. "I was hoping you'd say that."

"I'll cherish it forever."

"That's what I wanted to hear." He slipped the apron over her head, tied it and dropped a kiss on her cheek. "Why don't you chop up the vegetables while I prepare the lamb?"

"I—I can't. I haven't cooked since my mom died," she stammered, her heart threatening to beat out of her chest. "Every time I enter the bakery I relive the moment my mom slumped to the kitchen floor, moaning in pain, and I freeze up."

"Grace, I am so sorry for your loss. That must have been horrible."

"My friends and family think I should put the past behind me and resume baking, but I'm not strong enough. I just can't do it."

Jackson wrapped his arms around her, holding her tight. "Give yourself permission to grieve. It's the natural way of working through your pain and the only way to move forward."

His embrace made her feel comforted, as if she wasn't alone, and she adored him for it.

"Cry if you need to, yell, scream, do whatever it takes to feel better." His tone was full of compassion and sympathy. "And don't do anything you're not ready for, including baking."

"I miss creating new recipes and working with the staff, but I'm broken inside," she said, fighting the tears stinging her eyes. "I don't know how to live without her. My mom was my world, my everything, still is."

"Baby, you don't have to." Jackson rested a hand on her chest. "Your mom is right in here. In your heart. Forever. Her words are with you. Don't ever forget that."

Grace considered his advice. Jackson was right. Her mom *was* with her. She felt Rosemary's presence everywhere—at the bakery, at home, driving around town, even when she was at the gym. As he spoke, praising her for being strong in the face of adversity, her sadness lifted and her mood improved. Grace could always count on Jackson to make her feel better, to make her laugh and smile, and she appreciated his support.

"I want you to take it easy tonight. You've had a long week and you deserve to relax." Jackson swiped the remote control off the counter, handed it to Grace and gave her a peck on the lips. "You can deejay. Don't worry about dinner. I can handle it."

Feeling guilty, as if she was letting him down, she shook her head. "I can help. I'm fine."

"Trust me, I've got this."

"Have you cooked Indian food before?" she asked, noting the cookbooks strewn along the counter. "It's not as easy as it looks. Trust *me*. I learned the hard way several years ago."

"No, but I have all of the necessary ingredients, and as long as I follow Mariah's recipe to a T, everything will taste great." He added, "If it doesn't, I'll order a pizza!"

While Jackson cooked, they chatted about the Bite of Seattle festival, his brother's trip with his girlfriend to Snoqualmie Falls and Bronwyn's wedding.

Grace drummed her fingernails on the countertop, feeling restless and eager for something to do. Her eyes tracked Jackson around the kitchen, watching as he did his thing at the stove. He was a methodical cook, organized and exact in his approach, but Grace was so hungry she'd wolfed down an entire bag of carrots and feared dinner wouldn't be ready for hours.

"Cut the potatoes smaller. They'll cook faster," she advised. "And add more garlic to the soup. It will give the broth flavor and a rich, spicy taste."

Jackson nodded, but Grace knew he wasn't listening to her. He was too busy singing along with the radio, and his impersonation of the king of pop was so bad, Grace cupped her hands around her mouth and booed. "More cooking and less dancing."

He laughed, winking good-naturedly at her, and her heart swelled with happiness.

"Anything else, Ms. Bossy Pants?"

"Yes. Sprinkle some paprika on the lamb and don't forget the cumin. It's essential."

"Damn, you're worse than a backseat driver!"

"I wouldn't have to tell you what to do if you'd listen the first time."

"Since you're an expert, why don't you come over here and show me how it's done?"

"With pleasure!" Grace hopped off her stool, grabbed the wooden spoon from his hand and bumped him aside with her hip. "I've got this. Now, scram!"

Jackson raised his hands in the air and backed away from the stove. "I don't want any trouble. Just dinner!"

As Grace moved around the kitchen, happy images of her mom filled her mind. Rolling cinnamon buns. Icing cupcakes. Singing their favorite Cher song at the top of their lungs. Working side by side with Jackson, Grace realized she was creating wonderful new memories with him, and smiled to herself when he kissed her cheek for the second time in minutes. They talked about their families and past relationships, but Grace dodged his questions about Phillip. They were having a great time and she didn't want to ruin the night by discussing her ex.

"What qualities are you looking for in a guy?"

Grace turned off the stove. "He has to be thoughtful, sincere, loyal and romantic." Snapping her fingers, she fervently nodded. "And gainfully employed. If he doesn't have a j-o-b, he can't have me!"

"What's his name and what did he do?"

"What *didn't* he do?"

Jackson raised his eyebrows. "How did you meet?"

"Through friends. Phillip's brother was dating Bronwyn, so the four of us hung out a lot."

"Sounds cozy."

"It was. I met Phillip a couple months after my mom passed, and he helped fill the void in my life," Grace said sadly, with a heavy heart. "My dad told me Phillip was a gold digger who wanted to get his hands on my trust fund, but I didn't heed his warning."

"What went wrong?"

"Everything. He was a total gentleman when we first met, then he turned into a freakin' nightmare. He'd routinely ask for money and would give me the silent treatment if I refused. Phillip insisted on shopping and dining at premier restaurants, but expected me to pay."

Disgust darkened his face. "What a punk. You should have given him his walking papers the first time he asked you for money, because a real man would never mooch off his girl."

"That's not the worst of it."

"What could be worse than someone you love taking you for a ride?"

"Prior to meeting me, Phillip worked for the largest escort agency in Seattle."

Jackson whistled. "No shit. How did you find out about his past?"

"On my birthday. We ran into one of his 'friends' at the Hyatt, and their exchange piqued my curiosity. The woman was twice his age, dripping in diamonds, and practically threw herself at him. I did some digging, and thanks to Bronwyn I discovered the truth."

"Damn, that's terrible. I hope you dumped his ass, pronto."

"You know it! My mama didn't raise no fool." Yet Grace couldn't think about Philip without feeling like one. She couldn't believe how easily she'd believed his lies, and no longer trusted her own judgment. How could she have been so trusting and naive? If she could date the likes of Phillip Davies for nine months, what did that say about her?

Jackson uncorked the wine, filled two glasses and set them on a round silver tray.

"I can't believe how gullible I was," she complained, speaking her thoughts aloud. "I've always prided myself on being a smart, intelligent woman, but I never saw this coming."

"Don't beat yourself up. You did nothing wrong."

Eager to get the spotlight off of herself, she said, "Your turn. What do you want from a woman? Mind-blowing sex, ESPN privileges and a great steak?"

"Honesty, loyalty, and breakfast in bed from time to time would be nice."

"That's it?" Grace studied him, surprised by his confession. "You don't want much."

"I don't, but most of the women I meet are incapable of meeting my emotional and physical needs." Jackson wore a pensive expression on his face, as if his mind and heart were at odds, then shrugged. "I want to be with someone who understands me, and who I can trust. I want a lover and a best friend all rolled into one."

"Don't we all!" Grace picked up the salad bowl and patted Jackson affectionately on the cheek. "In the meantime, I'll settle for some help setting the table, so hurry up!"

Chapter 12

Candlelight flickered across the dining room, creating a romantic ambiance, but it was the sound of Grace's sultry laugh that put Jackson in an amorous mood. He couldn't take his eyes off her. He found himself remembering what they'd done last night at the Corbu Lounge and could almost hear her moans and groans in his ears now. It took every ounce of self-control he had to keep his hands in his lap and his butt in his seat.

"Thanks for inviting me over tonight." Grace stared at him over the rim of her glass, then took a sip of her wine. "You're great company, Jackson, and I enjoy spending time with you."

"And I with you, except when you're yelling at me in the kitchen!"

Grace gave him an exasperated look, as if she was annoyed with him, but Jackson could tell by her pursed lips that she was trying hard not to laugh.

"You should quit baking and take up acting. You're a natural! You'll win every award under the sun!

"Do you promise to be my leading lady?"

Grace beamed. "I'd love nothing more."

He raised her hand to his mouth and kissed it, allowing his lips to linger on her flesh. "That was the best meal I've had in a long time," he confessed, gesturing to his empty dinner plate. "You lied to me. You're not just a baker, you're an amazing cook, as well."

"Thanks, but I can't take all of the credit. My mom taught me everything I know about Indian cuisine, and if it wasn't for her patience and guidance I'd still be burning water!"

They laughed, moving closer to each other and intertwining fingers. Jackson yearned to love her, to stroke her body, wanted to make her scream his name. They'd made love every night that week, but since he didn't want Grace to think all he cared about was sex, he tore his gaze away from her mouth and deleted the explicit images from his mind.

Jackson was determined to keep his hands to himself, even if it killed him. They had more in common than just sex and he wanted to prove to Grace—and himself—that they could have fun outside of the bedroom. Though, if she made the first move he wouldn't stop her. Hell, who was he fooling? It would be a miracle if he made it through dessert without pouncing on her. Everything about Grace was a turn-on, and he wanted her every second of the day.

"How was practice?" she asked. "Is your team ready to defend their championship this season?"

"Not yet, but I'm confident they'll be in tip-top shape by opening night."

"That's because you're a great coach. The team is lucky to have you."

"I feel the same way about you." His hands were damp with sweat, cold and clammy, but he projected confidence. To Jackson, there was nothing better than being with Grace, and he wanted the world to know she was his girl. He moved closer to her, until their arms were touching. Feeling her warmth, her body against his, instantly calmed his nerves. "Diego's wife, Ana Sofia, is being honored at the Seattle Heritage Arts and Awards for her work with inner-city youth and I promised to attend the dinner to show my support. I know it's short notice, but I want you to be my date."

Jackson watched her, trying to gauge her reaction, but her expression was blank.

"If we attend the event together we'd be coming out publicly, so to speak," he continued, hoping he didn't sound as desperate as he felt. He wanted Grace by his side on Saturday night, didn't want to attend the event without her, and wished he'd asked her to be his date weeks ago instead of trying to hide their relationship from his friends and family. "Are you ready for that?"

"I think so," she said with a shy, endearing smile. "I can't wait to see you all dolled up, because your jeans-and-T-shirt look is getting a little tired!"

Jackson chuckled even though Grace was ribbing him about his wardrobe, and he didn't take offense. She'd said yes and that was all that mattered. "You sound like my mom."

"Is that a good thing or a bad thing?"

"That's a very good thing. I adore my mom and I'm not ashamed to admit it. My mother raised me to be a gentleman, taught me to appreciate, respect and protect women, and I wouldn't be the man I am today without her."

"Will your parents be at the awards show, as well?"

"No, they have a prior engagement, but you'll meet them, and the rest of my family, soon enough," Jackson promised, draping an arm around her shoulders. "I can't wait to show you off Saturday night. You're going to be the belle of the ball."

"And the females in attendance are *definitely* going to swoon over you."

"I don't care about anyone but you."

Her eyes smiled.

"I'm taking you to the Versace store this weekend. There's a red cut-out dress I have in mind for you and I know you're going to love it."

"You bake *and* shop?" she said, her tone filled with awe and wonder. "Be still, my heart. You *are* every woman's dream!"

They shared a laugh and another bottle of wine. Conversation was easy and comfortable, full of flirting, jokes and kisses, and Jackson realized for the first time in his life he was completely content with one woman, uninterested in every other girl. *Is Grace my future? Is she my soul mate? Can I trust her with my heart?* They'd only been dating for a few weeks, much too soon for him to declare his undying love, but he'd fallen hard for her. He didn't want to lose her to someone else, but instead of confessing his feelings, he snapped his mouth shut. Timing was everything, and Jackson didn't want to ruin their relationship by getting ahead of himself. He'd been burned before, betrayed by someone he'd cared deeply about, and was resolved to keep a lid on his emotions for now.

"I'm so excited about the roller derby tournament I'm counting down the days until I leave for Miami," Grace said, unable to sit still, practically bouncing up and down on her chair. "I'm psyched about it and so are my teammates."

"I want to hear all about it. When does it start? How long does it last?"

Animated and excited, Grace told him about the week-long competition on the east coast in August. "Last summer we got creamed, but not this year. If we work hard, we can win it all."

"You're going away for a week? That's a long time."

"You think so? I wanted to go for two weeks, but my teammates couldn't get the time off work. If I can convince Bronwyn to meet up with me, I'll definitely stay longer."

"Can I come?"

"As if!"

"Baby, I'm serious. I have plenty of vacation time, so let's make this trip happen."

Grace scoffed, dismissing his words with a flick of her hand. "You're all talk," she said, rolling her eyes to the ceiling. "We both know you're too busy with the bakery to join me in Miami, so drop the lovey-dovey act. You're not fooling anybody."

"What act? You're going to need something to do in the evenings, so why not *do* me?"

A smirk dimpled her cheeks and curled her lips. "Are you always this raunchy?"

"No, just when I'm with you."

Grace put the cover on the glass bowl and snapped it shut. "That's it," she quipped with a laugh. "No more rum truffles for you!"

The wall clock chimed and Jackson was surprised to see it was one in the morning. He lost track of time whenever Grace was around, and couldn't believe they'd been sitting in the dining room talking for three hours. Jackson couldn't recall ever being this enamored with a woman, but Grace Nicholas was the total package, and he loved spending time with her.

His gaze zeroed in on her, assessing her appearance. Her outfit was the perfect blend of naughty and nice, her dress so appealing he couldn't stop touching the soft material. Her mysterious aura made her irresistible, but it was her fiery wit that drew Jackson to her time and time again. Grace was a firecracker who kept him guessing, and just when he thought he'd figured her out she did something unexpected.

Jackson reflected on their relationship, could feel his grin widen as he remembered all the fun they'd had in recent weeks. Grace had treated him to a steak lunch one afternoon, surprised him with tickets to the football game at his alma mater after a rough day at the bakery and knocked his socks off when she'd shown up at his house in a black leather dress, sans underwear. Pushing him down on the couch, she'd freed his erection from his shorts, straddled him and rode him until he'd climaxed. She'd talked dirty to him, sucked and licked his ears as if they were coated in caramel and pumped her hips with more vigor than a horse jockey. Her behavior was outrageous, more explosive than a windmill dunk, and thinking about their fevered love-making made Jackson want more.

Sweat drenched his T-shirt, causing the lightweight material to cling to his skin. Thirsty, he picked up the water pitcher and filled his glass to the brim. Their eyes met, and time crawled to a stop. Desire flooded Jackson's body, leaving him speechless. His scalp tingled and blood shot to his groin. He'd seen that expression on her face before, knew exactly what Grace was thinking, what she wanted, what she needed, and made his move.

"Let's go upstairs," he proposed, rising to his feet. Her perfume washed over him, tickling his nostrils. She smelled like a tropical garden, fragrant and sweet, and her heady scent roused his senses. "I'll draw you a bath."

"You spoil me."

"I enjoy taking care of you. Are you complaining?"

"No, but I think it's time I return the favor."

"You're always doing nice things for me." To make her laugh, he patted her hips and joked, "But if you want to give me a massage, I won't object. You turned me out last night, and I have a crick in my neck to prove it!"

"I told you to lay still, but you wouldn't listen."

"You poured hot wax on my chest! What did you *expect* me to do!"

Giggling, she unbuckled his belt and unzipped his khaki pants.

"Grace, what are you doing?"

"Isn't it obvious? I'm thanking you for a wonderful evening."

Jackson pressed his eyes shut, groaned as her soft, delicate fingers seized his erection and worked their magic. His head fell back, rolled from side to side. It was impossible to think, to concentrate, when Grace was touching him, but he broke through the haze and met her eyes. "We've made love every night this week. Actually, every day since the first time in the locker room."

"Is that a problem?"

"No, but I don't want you to think all I care about is sex."

Her eyebrows rose and her lips parted in surprise, but she didn't speak.

"I want more than just your body, Grace. I want all of you. Your heart, your—"

Jackson heard the tremble in his voice, the vulnerability, and trailed off. He took a deep breath to steady his nerves, but it didn't help. His heart continued to pound in his ears, and his thoughts swirled like leaves in the wind. Why was it so hard for him to open up to her? Why couldn't he tell Grace the truth? That he'd fallen for her, and wanted them to be exclusive?

"Jackson, you're one of the sweetest, kindest people I've ever met, and I feel fortunate to have you in my life," she said. "I want you to know you're very special to me."

"I am? Prove it."

"I'm going to kiss you *here*," she said, stroking his shaft. "And you're going to love it."

Damn right I will. No one can ever compare to you.

"No shouting, okay, baby? I don't want your neighbors to call the cops again…"

Jackson cracked up. He'd never forget, for as long as he lived, the expression on Grace's face when Seattle's finest had showed up on his doorstep, demanding to have a look around. A week later, the incident still made him laugh.

"You know it's your fault the cops showed up, right?"

"If you say so," she cooed. "But *you're* the one who ripped off my dress and had your way with me."

Images from last Friday night filled his mind. They'd gotten carried away while playing poker, ended up having sex on the staircase and the next thing Jackson knew the cops were beating down his door. He'd done a lot of crazy things in his life, things he was ashamed of, but getting caught in the act with Grace wasn't one of them. They'd laughed about it, and made love again once the officers left.

"Jackson, you're right. I should leave before I get us in trouble—"

Grace spun around, but he grabbed her around the waist and pulled her to his chest. "You're not going anywhere. You're mine for the rest of the night."

"Just for tonight?" she whispered, brushing her lips against his mouth.

"How does forever sound?"

It wasn't a kiss; it was a sensuous assault. Grace devoured his mouth, kissing him with such hunger *his* knees buckled, and he slumped against the wall. Crushing her to him, he feasted on her lips, staked his claim with his tongue. It mated with hers, swirling and dancing around her minty fresh mouth.

Grace returned his kiss, matching his fire and intensity. He unzipped her dress, pushed it down her hips and tossed it aside, then made quick work of his clothes. Naked, their bodies pressed against each other, Jackson could feel desire radiating off her skin in waves. He sensed her excitement, how eager she was to please him, to love him, and sucked in a breath when she trailed kisses across his body, moving ever so slowly down his chest.

Licking his lips, he waited anxiously for Grace to make his fantasies a reality. She lowered herself to the floor, clutched his hips and drew his erection into her mouth, sucking it as if she was dying of thirst, and tingles stabbed his spine.

"Damn, baby, what are you doing to me?"

Grace twirled her tongue around the tip of Jackson's shaft, licking and teasing it. He sounded desperate, as if he was being tortured, but his face was covered in pleasure, the picture of pure bliss. Hearing his savage groans and grunts bouncing off the walls gave Grace a rush of adrenaline. She was the boss, in complete control, and it was a heady, exhilarating feeling.

Eager to please, she reached up and caressed his chest, tweaking his erect nipples. Having her way with him, calling the shots, was the ultimate turn-on. Grace decided right then and there, as Jackson thrusted himself deeper inside her mouth, that he was the only man for her, the only man she ever wanted to be intimate with. He was right about their relationship. It *was* about more than just great sex. They had great conversations, never ran out of topics to discuss, and confided in each other. More than anything, he made her feel supported, cherished, as if there was nothing he wouldn't do for her. The icing on the cake? The mind-blowing, toe-curling, earth-shattering sex. Jackson knew her body inside out, pleased her in every way, and no one would ever be able to take his place in the bedroom.

Gripping his shaft with her hands, she grazed her teeth along his length, nipping at it, licking and sucking. Grace enjoyed pleasing Jackson, loved being in control of his pleasure. He cupped her head, digging his nails into her hair, caressing and massaging her scalp.

"I don't know what I'd do if I lost you to someone else…"

Grace stared up at him, felt her eyes widen as he spoke openly about his deepest fears. Jackson was scared of losing her? Couldn't stomach the thought of seeing her with other guys? *But he's the one with numerous admirers, not me!* For some reason, his words turned her on, causing her to suck harder, faster, to lick his shaft as if it was a lollipop. Grace felt out of it, as if she was losing control.

Tremors shook Jackson's body and curses fell from his lips. His erection swelled inside her mouth, doubled in size, but he didn't climax. He yanked her to his chest and kissed her.

"Let's go upstairs." Soaking wet, desperate to feel him inside her, her body was vibrating with need. "I want you so bad it hurts."

"Screw it," he growled, lifting her onto the table. "I'm doing you right here, right now."

"No! You entertain in here, and—"

Jackson picked up his pants, retrieved a condom from the pocket and ripped it open. Within seconds, he rolled it onto his erection and positioned himself between her legs.

"You'll never be able to eat in here without thinking about us having sex."

A grin curled his lips. "I know. Isn't it great?"

"Baby, we can't do this. Your Chicago relatives are coming to visit at the end of the month and you're hosting a dinner party for them, remember?"

Jackson gave her a blank stare. "Yeah. So? What's the problem?"

"Let's go to your bedroom. We'll be more comfortable…"

Before Grace could finish her sentence, Jackson was inside her, moving, thrusting. She rocked against him, furiously pumping her hips. His hands explored her body, cupping and massaging her breasts, teasing her nipples with his thumbs, playing with the curls between her legs.

Passion swirled inside her, causing her to cry out. Kissing her, Jackson whispered sweet, soft words against her mouth. Clutching her hips, he dove into her, again and again and again.

"Deeper," she commanded, her words a breathless pant. "Deeper…faster…harder."

Jackson obliged, gave her everything she needed and more, moved his body with the skill of a trained dancer. "Baby, you like that? Is that what you want?"

"I don't like it—I love it… You're amazing."

Sweating profusely, her limbs sticky and hot, she stuck to his body like glue. Time passed with no end to their lovemaking in sight. It felt as if they'd been having sex for hours, but Grace didn't want Jackson to stop and told him she needed and wanted more. Grace couldn't get enough of him. She wanted to stay in his arms, loving him for the rest of the night. No one had ever loved her with such passion, and when Jackson hiked her legs in the air and sprayed kisses along her inner thighs, she lost it. Tingles tickled her spine and and an explosion erupted between her legs.

"Baby, turn around, I need you *bad*."

His command excited her, making her feel sexy and

desirable. Feeling weightless, lighter than air, Grace didn't have the energy to roll onto her stomach. It took supreme effort, but she focused her gaze on Jackson's face. His lips were moving, but Grace couldn't make out what he was saying. All she could hear was her erratic heartbeat ringing in her ears like a bell.

Inhaling sharply, Grace relished his scent. She'd lost her heart to Jackson the first time he'd ever kissed her, and weeks after Freezergate she was desperate for him, so turned on by their lovemaking she was chanting his name.

Her pulse quickened, and contractions rocked her body. Brilliant lights and colors exploded behind her eyes. A groan rose inside her throat, tumbling off her lips, as an orgasm reverberated through her core. It was heaven on earth, the cherry on top of the sundae, and she'd remember their thrilling, passionate night for the rest of her life.

The carnal pleasure of his kiss, the intensity of it, filled her with longing and desire. She raked her hands through his hair, clamped her legs possessively around his trim waist, met him thrust for thrust, proving she had the stamina to satisfy him.

"Damn, woman, are you trying to kill me?"

Satiated and sleepy, Grace closed her eyes and snuggled against him.

"Let's go upstairs. I have something to show you."

"Of course you do, but I need a nap before round two, so cool your heels, Drayson."

Chuckling, his hearty laugh filling the room, Jackson bent down, looped an arm around her waist and guided her up the staircase. In the master bedroom, he kissed her with such tenderness she melted against him and moaned into his mouth. And when they made love for the second time, wrapped up in each other's arms, Grace knew she'd never be the same again.

Chapter 13

Grace took the hand Jackson offered, stepped out of the Hummer limousine parked in front of the Marion Oliver McCaw Hall at Seattle Center and beamed when he pulled her close to his side, whispering compliments in her ear. It was early evening, but the air was still warm, the sun hot and the breeze humid. The wind carried the scent of flowers across the manicured grounds, and the soothing fragrance calmed Grace's nerves. Butterflies danced in her stomach, but one look at her handsome date and they dissipated.

"You're stunning, Grace, a vision of beauty," Jackson said proudly, his gaze sliding down her body. "I can't wait to get you home and rip this dress off of you."

"You paid big bucks for it, so I guess you can do what you want to it."

"Just the dress, or you, too?"

His touch along her hips made her heart soar and

her thoughts return to that afternoon. At three o'clock, he'd picked her up from the bakery—or rather a block away to avoid detection—and after hours of shopping they'd returned to his place to get ready for the awards dinner. But instead of getting dressed, they'd made love and consequently dozed off on the couch. If the limousine driver hadn't banged on the front door, waking them up, they'd still be fast asleep. It was a mad dash to get ready, but they'd left the house as scheduled. In the limousine, they'd laughed about their blunder, and thinking about how much fun they'd had that afternoon brought a girlish smile to her lips.

Gazing up at Jackson, Grace realized how much he meant to her. Their personalities complemented each other, they had great discussions about life and were open and honest with each other. Add to that, their chemistry was off the charts. Making love whenever the mood struck, whether they were washing his sports car, grilling in his backyard or taking a shower, was thrilling. And addictive. The more they had sex, the more Grace wanted him, and when he brushed his lips against her cheek she imagined herself pushing him back inside the limo, hiking up her dress and climbing on top of him.

"You look so sexy I won't be able to keep my hands off you."

"Likewise," she quipped, admiring his stylish attire. Jackson looked sharp in his navy blue suit, white shirt and striped Burberry tie, but his boyish smile was his best accessory. "I hope no one sinks their claws into you when I'm not looking."

"That will never happen." Cupping her chin, he

brushed his lips softly against her mouth. "I only have eyes for you."

Good, because I feel the same way. I don't want anyone but you.

Arms intertwined, they strode along the walkway, admiring the spectacular view of the Space Needle. McCaw Hall was decorated with colored lights, creating an ethereal ambiance, and fashionably dressed guests posed for pictures on the red carpet.

Open and inviting, the lobby was decorated with a tornado-like chandelier, attractive art pieces and high-end furniture. Servers, decked out in formal attire, carried trays of champagne and appetizers, and Jackson and Grace enjoyed sampling the complimentary food and beverages.

"Jackson Drayson, is that you?"

Grace spotted a voluptuous blonde in a black cocktail gown making eyes at Jackson, and narrowed her gaze. The woman had a Nokia camera in one hand and a cocktail glass in the other, and was smiling bright.

"Good evening," Jackson said, frowning. "Do I know you?"

The smile slid off her lips. "It's me. Delilah. Delilah Hasani…"

He wore a blank expression.

"We hung out in Miami last year. No, it was Vegas!" she shrieked, speaking a mile a minute. "I was working at the MGM Grand, and you were watching a boxing match with your friends. Or, was it the NBA finals? Geez, Louise, I can't remember…"

Listening to the blonde, her amusement growing, Grace sipped her champagne. She had nothing to worry about. The woman was no competition, and it was obvious Jackson was bored. He was staring at *her*, not the chatty stranger, and tightened his hold on her waist.

"If my memory serves me correctly, you're a flight attendant, right?" he asked.

"Your memory sucks! I'm a freelance photographer and I'm here on assignment."

"My bad," Jackson said in a contrite voice. "See you around. Don't work too hard—"

"How about a picture? You're a striking pair, definitely magazine-worthy."

"You're right. My girlfriend is stunning, isn't she?"

Jackson moved in close and kissed Grace on the cheek, causing her to giggle.

"One, two, three," the blonde counted from behind the camera lens.

The bulb flashed and after thanking Delilah, they continued through the lobby.

McCaw Hall was packed, filled with some of the most influential people in Seattle, and Grace hoped she didn't run into Ainsworth or his high-and-mighty parents. To please her father, she'd agreed to have lunch with the businessman on Monday afternoon, and Grace was dreading it. It was *her* life, and she had to stop letting her dad boss her around. Last week, she'd found a Realtor and was fervently searching for her dream place, somewhere she could call her own.

Entering the bright and spacious auditorium, they were greeted by a balding usher who led them to their first-tier seats. Walking down the aisle on Jackson's arm made Grace feel like a celebrity. People stared and gawked, and she knew every woman in the room wished they could trade places with her. Grace didn't blame them. Jackson was a catch, a perfect gentleman with a great personality and a big heart. He planned romantic dates for her, and surprised her with gifts when she least expected it. Sure, they disagreed at times, and argued about hot-button issues, but Grace wanted a future with Jackson, and hoped they could overcome their differences—namely her father. She'd planned to talk to him last night at dinner, but she'd lost her nerve when he'd badmouthed Lillian's bakery. Her dad was going out of town tomorrow to visit a sick friend in Spokane, but when he returned she'd come clean about her relationship with Jackson. Grace hoped he wouldn't lose his temper, or worse, disown her. The thought made her heart ache—

"Grace, I want you to meet Diego and his wife, Ana Sofia," Jackson said, clapping his friend on the back. "They cheat at poker, but they're still one of my favorite couples!"

"It's wonderful to meet you both and congratulations on your award, Ana Sofia."

Shaking hands with the couple, Grace noted how affectionate they were toward each other, and instantly liked them. Seated in his wheelchair at the end of the aisle, Diego gazed up at his wife with love in his eyes, and she was beaming at him.

"Thank you, Grace. It's great to finally put the name to a face, and what a beautiful face it is." Ana Sofia patted Jackson's cheek. "This guy's family, so take good care of him, okay?"

"I'll try my best, Ana Sofia, but I'm not going to lie. He's a handful!"

Chuckling, Diego fervently nodded. "Tell me something I don't know!"

The lights dimmed in the auditorium and the master

of ceremonies appeared on stage. Promising to meet up later during dinner, the couples took their seats.

"Your friends seem nice—"

"I'm a handful, huh?" Jackson whispered in her ear, his voice filled with mischief. "Wait until we get home. I'll show you just how *bad* I can be."

Grace was blown away. Not with the designer table linens or elaborate flower arrangements beautifying the Allen Foundation for the Arts room, but by how spectacular the awards show had been. Awards had been handed out, speeches had been made and the performances had moved Grace to tears. And now guests were ready to party.

Hunger pains stabbed Grace's stomach. A tantalizing aroma tickled her nose and she wet her lips in anticipation, knowing the food would be plentiful and delicious. Seated at a table with Ana Sofia, Diego and their family members, Grace laughed at their outrageous stories.

"Do you want something from the bar?" Jackson asked, gently rubbing her back.

"Yes, please. I'd love a strawberry daiquiri."

"I'm worried about getting you another alcoholic drink."

Puzzled, Grace gave him a sideways glance. "Why?"

"You know how you get when you drink," he whispered.

"No, I don't. How do I get?"

"Buck wild!"

Laughing, Grace snatched her napkin off the table and threw it at him.

"You look all sweet and innocent, but after a couple cocktails you turn into a freak."

"I do not," she argued, speaking only loud enough for him to hear.

"You're right. My bad. I must be confusing you with someone else." He cocked his head to the right, as if deep in thought, and stroked the length of his jaw. "Though you look a *lot* like the woman who jumped me in the shower and had her way with me this afternoon."

Her body flushed with heat as memories of their fervent lovemaking filled her mind. Grace stared at Jackson, thinking she'd jump him again in a heartbeat.

"Diego, go with Jack," Ana Sofia insisted, flapping her bejewelled hands in the air. "I want a vodka tonic and some more caviar, so please track down a server."

The men left and Ana Sofia wasted no time grilling Grace about Jackson. How did they meet? Were they in love? Were they going to get married? The high school art teacher had an infectious personality, and Grace enjoyed chatting with her, but dodged her intrusive questions.

"When Diego told me Jack was serious about someone, I didn't believe him," she confessed. "I've known Jack for years, but you're the only woman I've ever seen him fawn over and it's adorable. He's really into you, Grace, and it's great to see."

"But he was engaged before—"

"Yeah, but Mimi proposed, and it's not true love if the woman pops the question."

Grace laughed. "Really? Says who?"

"My *abuela*, and she's *never* wrong."

"Why did they break up?" she asked, filled with curiosity. "Was he unfaithful?"

Sadness touched her features. "No, he dumped Mimi because she—"

"Congratulations on your award, Ana Sofia!" a woman interrupted. "Everyone at Lakeside Upper School is thrilled for you. You're a shining example of what one can accomplish with dedication, perseverance and hard work..."

Several couples joined them, chatting excitedly about Ana Sofia's award, and Grace checked out of the conversation, instead searching the room for Jackson. She found him standing at the bar with a dark-skinned beauty of African descent, and rolled her eyes to the ceiling. What the hell? Did he have to flirt with everyone in the room? Had he forgotten that she was his date?

The woman placed a hand on his chest and Grace suspected they had been lovers. Her heart dropped and her shoulders sagged. Was there anyone in Seattle he hadn't slept with? Was she fooling herself? Would Jackson ever be able to commit to her, or would she always have to compete with the masses for his attention?

Needing a distraction, Grace took her cell phone out of her purse and scrolled through her newest text messages. Bronwyn wanted to have drinks tomorrow night, her dad had sent a message reminding her about Monday's staff meeting and Ainsworth wanted her to call him.

Her gaze wandered, landing again on Jackson. Grace strangled a groan as yet another woman was breathing down his neck. This one was tall, all boobs and ass, with a curly weave flowing down her back.

Hurling her cell into her purse, Grace considered leaving, but before she could head for the nearest exit Jackson was at her side, offering the cocktail she'd requested.

"Here you go."

"Took you long enough." Grace regretted the quip the moment it left her mouth. She sounded pitiful, and cringed with shame when Jackson gave her a puzzled look. Grace hated seeing him with other women, wanted him all to herself, but knew it would never be. This was their "coming out" party, not their engagement party, and she didn't want to ruin their date by acting possessive. "I shouldn't have said that. It's none of my business who you talk to."

He took her hands in his and kissed them. "Baby, it's not like that. Tanisha and Zoey are old friends, and nothing more. I asked you to be my date tonight because I wanted to show you off to the world. You're my girl, and don't you forget it."

Grace snuggled against him, enjoying his tender caress across her skin.

"You're gorgeous, you know that? The most beautiful woman in the room…"

Moved by his words, and the sincerity of his expression, she rested a hand on his face. As she leaned forward to kiss Jackson, a couple caught her eye and she froze. The woman in the silver, backless, gown was old enough to be Grace's mother, but it was the expression on the man's face that made Grace want to laugh. Phillip looked bewildered, as if he couldn't believe what he was seeing. His eyes were saucers, his mouth was wide open, and when he stumbled over his feet he spilled champagne on his tacky powder-blue suit.

Ignoring him, Grace closed her eyes and pressed her lips against Jackson's. It was a perfect kiss, fraught with passion and desire, and her body responded enthusiastically to him. Jackson pulled away before she'd had her fill of him, but Grace knew they'd have plenty of time to make love later and smiled at the thought.

"You're stunning and I want everyone to know you're mine," he murmured against her ear, his tone thick with desperation. "May I have this dance?"

His cologne wafted over her, ticking her flesh, exciting her like his kiss as he stood to his feet.

Feeling sexy, desirable and hot, Grace rose from her chair, and coiled an arm around his. "I thought you'd never ask," she said, unable to wipe the smile off her face.

"Are you having fun?"

"Absolutely. Thanks for inviting me, Jackson. I'm having a great time."

"That makes two of us. Now, let's show everyone how to get down and dirty!"

As Jackson took her in his arms and kissed her passionately on the lips, Grace wished their wonderful, magical night together would never end.

Chapter 14

"I thought you'd never get back." Jackson watched Mariah breeze into the bakery kitchen, smiling from ear to ear, and knew she'd been with Everett. These days the couple spent all their free time together, and it amazed him how girly his sister acted whenever her millionaire fiancé was around. "Where did Lover Boy take you for lunch?"

Mariah washed her hands in the sink and dried them with a tea towel. "The Sheraton, and my five-course meal was to die for, especially the dessert. White truffles are my favorite!"

"Is *that* why you've been gone for three hours?"

"Two, but who's counting?" she replied, smirking.

Jackson laughed. He couldn't believe how much his sister had changed since meeting Everett three months earlier. The businessman brought out the best in Mariah, made her smile like no one else, and Jackson admired the single dad for being an honest, stand-up guy.

"My turn. I'm starving." Jackson took off his apron, dropped it on the counter and lowered the temperature on the oven. "Do you mind checking on the mocha soufflés and whipping up another batch of raspberry scones? I was going to, but things got crazy after you left and Kelsey asked me to come out front and lend a hand."

"No, problem, Jack. Take as long as you need."

"Okay," he said with a wink. "See you in three hours!"

Jackson grabbed his BLT from the fridge and left the kitchen. Remembering he hadn't responded to Chase's earlier message, he sent his brother a text. Chase and Amber were finally back in Seattle and en route to the bakery. He couldn't believe his brother—the self-proclaimed workaholic who was obsessed with planning and strategizing— had actually taken a vacation. More shocking still, Jackson had met Grace and dumped every other girl. He wanted a future with Grace, could see them living together in wedded bliss, but he wanted to talk things over with Chase before he made any rash decisions. Grace was busy at the bakery—her earlier texts had said as much—but Jackson wanted to hear her voice. He dialed her cell number, waiting anxiously for her to pick up, but the call went straight to voice mail. "Baby, it's me. Call me when you get this. Love you…"

Jackson stared at his cell phone in disbelief, amazed at his bold declaration. He sat there for several seconds, thinking about what he'd done, and wondered what Grace would think when she heard his message. He'd never said "I love you" before, hadn't planned on blurting it out, but he didn't regret his confession. It was true. He *did* love her, and he wasn't afraid to admit it.

His stomach groaned and he tasted the sandwich Grace had made for him that morning. Jackson liked her being at his place, loved coming home to her at the end of the day, and wanted her around permanently. They cooked together, spent hours cuddled up on the couch watching TV, listening to music and playing board games. He couldn't imagine being with anyone else, and as Jackson reflected on the past few weeks he realized he was more positive and enthusiastic about life, and Grace was the reason why. She was the strongest woman he knew, not to mention the most beautiful, and Jackson wanted to grow old with her.

"I thought you could use a drink, so I brought you a mango lemonade. Enjoy!"

Jackson broke free of his thoughts, noticed the glass on the table and smiled at the fresh-faced barista. "Thanks, Kelsey. You're one in a million."

The intern beamed. "Anytime, boss. Holler if you need anything else."

Picking up the discarded newspaper on the table, he skimmed the headlines. Jackson flipped open the paper and his sandwich fell from his hands. He froze, as his gaze zeroed in on the advertisement on page two. "What the hell?" Sweetness Bakery had taken out a full-page ad for their new dessert, Chocolate Explosion, and it looked similar…no, exactly like the Draynut. Different name, but he'd bet every dollar in his bank account it tasted the same.

Jackson was so engrossed in his thoughts, gazing intently at the advertisement, he didn't realize Chase,

Amber and Mariah were standing beside his table until his sister waved her hands in front of his face.

Closing the newspaper, Jackson jumped to his feet and hugged the happy couple. He was pissed, but he forced a smile on his lips and spoke in a jovial tone. Until he spoke to Grace, he had to hide the truth about their relationship and the stolen recipe from his siblings. That, or go into hiding. "Welcome home," he said, clapping his brother on the back. "How was your trip? Did you have a good time?"

Chase wrapped his arms around Amber. "I was with my number-one girl. What do you think?"

"I wanted to stay another week, but duty calls," Amber said with a shrug.

"We had a great time, but it's good to be home." A frown darkened Chase's eyes, causing worry lines to wrinkle his forehead. "Trouble's brewing, and if we don't launch a counterattack we could be out of business by the end of the year."

Alarmed, perspiration wet his skin. Had Chase seen the ad in the *Seattle Times*?

Chase's next words confirmed he had. "Sweetness is advertising their new dessert on billboards all over town."

Mariah gasped. "On billboards? How can they afford that? They're super expensive."

"That's not the worst of it. Unfortunately, there's more…"

Jackson groaned inwardly, hanging his head as he listened to his brother discuss the radio advertisement he'd heard for Sweetness Bakery as he was driving to Lillian's minutes earlier.

"They're going all out to promote Chocolate Explosion because Bite of Seattle is next week," Chase explained. "They're trying to prove they're the best bakery in town, but they're not. That's why they're resorting to dirty tricks."

"This is wrong! How could they do this? They stole our recipe!"

In a state of shock, Jackson couldn't speak.

"What did you tell Grace about the Draynut?" Shouting her words, Mariah leveled a finger at him. "Did you show her the recipe? Is that how this happened?"

"Of course not! I'd never do that—"

"Then how did Sweetness get my recipe?" she demanded.

Amber frowned, scratching her head. "I'm lost. Who's Grace?"

"Jack's new girlfriend."

"Good one, Mariah." Chase chuckled. "No, really, who is she?"

"Jack met Grace Nicholas a couple days after you left for your trip, and he's been wooing her ever since. He took her to the Heritage Awards last Saturday, and the next morning their picture was splashed all over the internet and the local newspapers."

Chase scoffed. "Get out of here. You can't be serious. Jack does booty calls, not romantic dates."

"Chase, I wish I was. I told him to stop seeing her, but he wouldn't listen, and now look. She stole the Draynut recipe and screwed us over."

"No, she didn't," Jackson replied, annoyed that his sister was making false accusations about his girlfriend. Doubts crowded his mind, but he spoke with confidence. "Grace would never betray me, and furthermore, she's never been in the back of the shop."

"Of course she has! You guys got locked inside the storage room, remember, lover boy?"

"What?" Chase roared, his voice reverberating around the room. "Jack, are you out of your mind? How could you have done something so stupid? Are you trying to ruin us?"

Wearing a shaky smile, her gaze darting around the bakery, Amber clutched Chase's forearm and spoke quietly to him. "Baby, not here. Let's go talk in the kitchen."

Determined to get to the bottom of things, Jackson swiped his cell phone and the newspaper off the table. "I'll be back later."

Mariah slid in front of him to thwart his escape, but Jackson stepped past her.

"Where are you going?" Chase asked.

"To uncover the truth."

Jackson tried calling Grace from the car as he sped towards Sweetness Bakery, but her voice mail came on again. Why wasn't she answering her phone? They texted each other all day long, spoke on the phone, too, and he couldn't recall a time when he couldn't reach her.

Arriving at Sweetness Bakery, he found parking across the street. It was a small brick building, but what it lacked in size it more than made up for in character. Colorful signs and pictures hung in the front window, a chalkboard displayed the menu and a barista in a pumpkin costume stood in front of the store offering pedestrians sweet treats.

Standing at the intersection, waiting impatiently for the light to change, Jackson took off his sunglasses and stared through the shop window. No, he wasn't seeing things. Grace was sitting at a table with a buff, blond-haired man. It was her. No doubt about it. He recognized her outfit. That morning, as they were leaving his house, he'd complimented her, told her how beautiful she looked in her peach-colored dress, and she'd thanked him with a kiss.

Seeing Grace with another man was a shock to his system, leaving him dazed and confused. Is that why she wasn't answering his calls? Because she was too busy hanging out with G.I. Joe? All at once it hit him. The truth. The real reason Grace was spending time with him—so she could steal his family recipes.

Feeling stupid for ever trusting her, his heart ached with sadness. Looking back, Jackson realized he'd made a mistake befriending her. *What was I thinking? Why didn't I keep my distance? Guard my heart?*

Glancing up the road to ensure the coast was clear, Jackson jogged across the street and into Sweetness Bakery, anger shooting through his veins. Grace was so busy flirting with her tanned, blue-eyed date she didn't notice he'd entered the shop.

Didn't notice, or didn't care? his conscience jeered.

Jackson didn't know what he was angrier about—Grace stealing the Draynut recipe, or him catching her with another man. The latter, he decided, stalking toward the largest table inside the bright, sweet-smelling shop. "You guys look cozy," he said, faking a smile.

Her eyes widened, but Grace spoke in a calm voice. "Jackson, what are you doing here?"

"We need to talk *now*."

"This is not a good time."

"Why? Because you're busy cheating on me with this clown?"

Grace glared at him, as if *he* was the one out of line, and rose to her feet.

"How long has this been going on?"

G.I. Joe tossed his napkin on the table. "Who are you and what do you want?"

"I don't think we've met. I'm Jackson Drayson. Grace's boyfriend."

The color drained from the man's face and he coughed into his fist.

"Ainsworth, please excuse me. I'll be right back."

Jackson slid his hands into his pockets, didn't move, although Grace gestured for him to follow her. Everyone in the shop was staring at them but Jackson didn't care. He wasn't leaving until Grace told him the truth about the stolen Draynut recipe and her blond lover boy.

"Baby, let's talk outside," she whispered, giving him a pleading look. "It's not what you think, and you're getting worked up over nothing."

Grace reached for him, trying to touch his arm, but Jackson moved away.

"We can talk here. I have nothing to hide. Do you?"

"Jackson, please." Her gaze darted around the shop. "You're making a scene."

"Of course I'm making a scene! You betrayed me."

"Ainsworth is a family friend," she explained. "He's not my man. *You* are."

"Not anymore. We're through."

Her face fell and her bottom lip quivered.

"Dating you was a mistake. I don't know what I was thinking—"

"Where is this coming from… What did I do wrong?"

"Everything!" he shouted, unable to govern his temper. Jackson reached into his back pocket and pulled out the crumpled newspaper ad. "Did you think I wouldn't see this? That I was too stupid to put two and two together."

Grace stared at the advertisement, her eyes wide.

"I never should have befriended you, or taken a chance on love." Jackson knew he was shouting, heard the disgust in his voice, the pain, but he couldn't control his emotions. "You set me up and I was too blind to see it."

Tears filled her eyes. "That's not true! I didn't pursue you. *You* pursued me."

"And you made sure to capitalize on that, didn't you?

"I had nothing to do with this campaign and I didn't steal the Draynut recipe."

Her denial did nothing to soothe his feelings. Her words meant nothing to him. Guilt was written all over her face, clear to see, and Jackson knew his suspicions were right. "Tell me the truth. You owe me at least that."

"I just did."

"You won," he said with a shrug of his shoulders. "Happy now?"

"Baby, wait. Let's talk about this! We can fix this!"

With a heavy heart, Jackson turned and marched through the shop and out the door.

Grace called out to him, yelling his name, but he didn't look back.

Chapter 15

Grace opened the industrial oven inside the bakery kitchen, took out the metal pan with one hand and the cookie tray with the other. Since arriving at the shop at 5:00 a.m. that morning she'd baked dozens of mocha brownies, apple-cranberry tarts and hazelnut cookies, and although she'd been on her feet for hours Grace felt invigorated, not tired. Cooking dinner with Jackson weeks earlier had reminded Grace how much she loved being in the kitchen. She was devastated about their breakup, but she found comfort in baking her mother's favorite recipes.

To take her mind off Jackson she'd cleaned the shop from top to bottom, finished her monthly financial report and made her hard-working employees a continental breakfast when they'd arrived to work. The more Grace baked, the less upset she was.

Her thoughts returned to Monday afternoon. Jackson had marched into the bakery shouting accusations at her, and Grace shivered in horror at the memory of their argument. She'd felt as if she was in the eye of the storm and didn't know how to save herself. His insults had pierced her soul, broken her heart in two. With tears in her eyes, she'd watched Jackson storm out of the shop, jump into his car and speed off.

Forty-eight hours later, Grace still couldn't make sense of what had gone wrong, of how she'd lost the man she loved. She'd called Jackson numerous times over the last two days, but to no avail. After hearing his voice mail, and the words *I love you* fall from his mouth, she'd decided to go to his house. If not for Bronwyn talking her out of it, she would have driven to his place and forced him to talk to her. But that wasn't the answer. As much as she loved Jackson, and wanted to be with him, she was scared he'd hurt her, and didn't know what she'd do if he rejected her again. She felt sick over their argument, but Grace didn't know how to make things right.

Grace thought about her solitary breakfast that morning at home. She'd decided to write Jackson a letter, but crumpled it up and started over several times. Grace was hurt by his accusations, couldn't believe Jackson thought so little of her. She teared up as she remembered the hurtful things he'd said. Filled with sadness and despair, she'd changed her mind about reaching out to him. There was nothing to say. All she could do was learn from the situation, and move on with her life because Jackson hated her and he wasn't coming back.

Her phone buzzed and Grace fished it out of her apron pocket, hoping her new text message was from

Jackson. It wasn't. Disappointed, she slumped against the counter. She knew Bronwyn meant well, but her incessant quotes about love and hardships were depressing. Grace didn't need anyone to remind her she'd lost Jackson; the pain was constant, all-consuming, would be with her forever.

Grace pressed her eyes shut. Policing her thoughts, she chose not to dwell on her failed relationship with Jackson, or the promises they'd made to each other. Gathering herself, she wiped at her cheeks with the sleeve of her blouse. She didn't have time to cry. She had a bakery to run and couldn't spend the rest of the day hiding out in the kitchen having a pity party for one.

Her gaze landed on the black-and-white photograph hanging beside the kitchen door. Her mom was glowing in the image, beaming like a bride on her wedding day, and Grace owed it to her mom to pull herself together, and get back to work. She felt her mother's spirit around her, her aura, could hear her voice in her ears now and wanted to make her proud.

Entering the shop, holding the pastry trays, Grace smiled and greeted customers. It turned out Jackson was right. Chatting with the regulars, hearing their heartfelt stories about Rosemary, was uplifting, and Grace drew strength from their memories and words of encouragement.

"It's good to see you back in the kitchen!" a cop said with a broad smile.

"Welcome back, dear. We've missed you," an elderly woman exclaimed.

A mother of three whooped for joy. "I'll have a dozen

of your maple almond squares. I've *really* missed your baking!"

Grace glanced at the door and her stomach coiled into a knot. She thought the gentleman waiting in line was Jackson, but when she realized it wasn't, tears filled her eyes for the second time in minutes. *Get it together, Grace. You're losing it.* Taking a deep breath helped steady her nerves. The moment passed and she made quick work of replenishing the display shelves.

"Pumpkin, is that you?"

Hearing her dad's voice, Grace turned toward the kitchen. His eyes were bright, and seeing his toothy smile lifted her spirits and warmed her heart. "Hey, Dad! Welcome home."

"I heard you were in the kitchen baking up a storm, but I had to come see for myself." He kissed her forehead. "You couldn't have picked a better time to dust off your oven mitts. Bite of Seattle starts on Friday, and with you back at the helm we're going to crush the competition."

"Dad, we need to talk."

"Not now, pumpkin, I have an important meeting across town and I'm late."

"But you just got here." Recognizing she was being insensitive, Grace asked about his trip to Spokane. "How is Mr. Baldwin doing? Is he still in the hospital?"

"Yes, but the doctors expect him to make a full recovery," he explained. "Maybe next time I go visit, you can come."

"Sure, Dad. I'd like that. Mr. Baldwin is a sweet old man who tells great stories."

"I have to run. I forgot my briefcase so I dropped by to pick it up, but I can't stay."

Grace trailed her dad through the shop and down the hallway, speed-walking to keep up with him. No easy feat in a pencil skirt and high heels, but Grace wasn't letting him out of her sight until he came clean about the Chocolate Explosion. She'd sampled one yesterday, and sure enough it tasted like the Draynut. Did her dad have spies working at Lillian's? Had he paid someone to swipe the recipe? Were there others he planned to steal and pass off as his own?

"Dad, did you plant spies at Lillian's to steal the Draynut recipe?"

"You think they're the only ones who are creative?" A snarl curled his lips. "Well, they're not. Our staff worked damn hard creating the Chocolate Explosion, but you'd know that if you'd been here, instead of running around town with that Drayson boy."

Anguish squeezed her heart at the sound of Jackson's name.

"I had to hear about your relationship on the street!" Sadness flickered in his eyes, darkening his face, and his voice broke. "Do you have any idea how that made me feel?"

"Dad, I'm sorry. I was going to tell you, but it was never the right time—"

"You have no business dating that boy. He's a scoundrel just like Phillip."

"They're nothing alike. Jackson has a career, his own money and life goals."

"Why can't you date someone like Ainsworth? His family is worth *billions*."

"Good for them," she replied angrily. "I don't want Ainsworth. We have nothing in common."

He flapped his hands in the air, dismissing her words.

"Nonsense. You have everything in common. You're both smart, hard-working people from good families."

"Jackson is the only man I want. If I can't have him, I don't want anyone."

"I don't trust him, so break things off."

"It's over between us…" Saying the words aloud wounded her afresh. Jackson's face haunted her dreams at night, and she'd woken up that morning, longing to be back in his arms. "Jackson found out about the stolen Draynut recipe and he dumped me."

"Good. It makes things easier. Now you won't have to choose between us."

Stunned by his words, Grace stared at him in astonishment. She was done. Through letting her dad control her, and knew if she didn't take a stand now she'd never be independent.

He'd always warned her about men who'd try to take advantage of her, but she'd never imagined he'd be the one to hurt her the most. "I'm moving out of the house. It's time."

"But Grace—"

"But nothing, Dad. This is long overdue."

"Pumpkin, you can't go. I need you."

"And I need my independence, my freedom," she insisted, standing her ground. "If I don't move out you'll always treat me like a little girl, instead of a grown woman with a life of her own."

"Where is this coming from? Did the Drayson boy put you up to this?"

Filled with empathy, her heart overflowing with love, Grace wore a sympathetic smile. "Dad, I'm not leaving you. I'm spreading my wings, just like you did when you were my age."

"Fine, do what you want, but don't come running to me when you fall flat on your face."

"I won't," she said, meeting his gaze. "You and Mom have given me all the tools I need to be successful in life, and I won't let you down."

"Are you leaving Sweetness, too, or just me?"

"I'm committed to this shop, this community and our customers, and that won't change."

He released an audible sigh. "That's good to hear. And now that we have the Chocolate Explosion we can finally crush those jerks at Lillian's."

Seeing his narrowed gaze and the smug I'm-the-man expression on his face bothered her. Something clicked in Grace's mind, and she sensed her suspicions were right. He *had* planted someone at Lillian's. He'd never admit it to her, but it didn't matter. The writing was on the wall, and knowing her father was responsible for hurting the man she loved made Grace feel sick to her stomach. Sadly, things like this had happened before. Since her mother's death, she'd heard rumblings that her dad had engaged in dirty tactics to stay on top, but she'd ignored the rumors.

Not anymore. "I want to expand the business, and build shops nationwide, but if you steal another recipe from Lillian's, I'll quit."

"All's fair in love and war, *and* business."

"Mom wouldn't want this. If she was alive she'd be ashamed of you for stealing from our competitors." Grace couldn't hide her disgust. "And so am I."

Shame passed over his features, but Grace didn't stick around to hear his apology. Spinning around on her heels, she fled the office, willing the tears in her eyes not to fall.

Chapter 16

"I can't do this. I can't sit here and pretend everything's hunky-dory when I'm pissed…"

Utensils dropped, clanging against gold-rimmed plates, and an awkward silence fell across Graham and Nadia's lavishly decorated dining room. A couple of times a month, the Drayson family met for dinner, and although Jackson was miserable, he'd driven to his folks' place after his afternoon workout with his friends, hungry for his mother's delicious cooking.

"I'm so angry I feel like hitting something," Mariah continued, shouting her words.

Jackson closed his gaping mouth. His sister never raised her voice, so he was stunned by her outburst. "Sis, what's wrong? Did you and Everett have an argument or something?"

"No," she snapped, pointing her fork at him. "I'm mad at you."

"Me? What did I do?"

Mariah surged to her feet. "You screwed Lillian's over and that's not okay."

"Jack, Mariah, what's going on?" Nadia asked. "What's this all about?"

"Jack hooked up with our biggest competitor."

Eyebrows raised, his parents exchanged a worried look, and Jackson dropped his gaze to his plate. *Damn. Do we have to do this now? Can't I eat in peace?* Four days ago, his world had come crashing down around him, and he was still coming to terms with what had happened. Jackson tried to block the incident from his mind, but it didn't work. He'd fallen victim to anger on Monday, but now that he'd had time to reflect on his argument with Grace, he had doubts about her guilt. Snitching to her father was out of character for her. She wasn't the sneaky, deceptive type, and she didn't have a calculating bone in her body.

Remembering the things he'd said to her filled Jackson with shame. He only had himself to blame for his problems. *What have I done? Why didn't I give her a chance to explain instead of going off half-cocked? Is it too late to make amends?* Deciding it wasn't, he formulated a plan. Winning back Grace was a daunting task, but Jackson was up for the challenge. He wanted a future with her, needed her in his life, and didn't want to live another day without her. Nothing was going to keep them apart. Not even his family—

His mother's shrill voice cut into his thoughts and Jackson wondered how long he'd been daydreaming about Grace.

"Jack, is this true?" Even at home, surrounded by family, Nadia's makeup was perfect, every hair was in place and her floral designer dress was fresh off the Paris runway. "Have you been sleeping with the enemy?"

He dodged his mother's gaze, and her question. "Grace would never do the things Mariah is accusing her of."

"How would you know?" Chase asked. "It's not as if you guys are in a committed relationship. It's just sex. Three months from now you won't even remember her name."

"Chase, shut up. It isn't like that. Grace is different."

"Are you trying to sabotage the bakery?" Mariah asked.

"What kind of question is that?"

"A fair one," his brother argued. "Of all the women in Seattle you choose to hook up with our competitor. Why? Don't you have enough excitement in your life already?"

"You're a fine one to talk. You hooked up with the help."

Chase looked sour, and Jackson regretted taking a cheap shot at his big brother.

"Keep Amber out of this. She didn't steal the Draynut recipe—your booty call did."

Jackson shook his head. "This isn't fair. You guys both found love at Lillian's, so why are you ganging up on me for dating someone I met at the bakery?" His question was met with silence and Jackson knew he'd given his siblings something to think about. "I trust Grace. It's just not in her to be sneaky and deceitful."

His sister rolled her eyes to the ceiling, infuriating him, but Jackson fought back.

"You run the bakery, Mariah. Not me."

"What's that supposed to mean?"

"I'm not a puppet. I'm my own man," he said coolly. "I do what's best for me, not what you tell me to do, so back off."

"We're supposed to be a team!" Chase stood beside Mariah. "Have you forgotten that?"

Rising to his feet, he glared at his brother. "We are a team. I bust my butt every day to ensure everything runs smoothly at Lillian's, so don't you dare question my loyalty and dedication to the bakery."

"Then why did you tell her our secrets?" Mariah asked. "Who knows what else she's told her father about us, or how many other recipes she swiped when you weren't looking."

Chase wore a menacing look on his face. "You're jeopardizing our business, our reputations and our family name by sneaking around town with that woman."

His hands curled into fists. "Her name is Grace—"

"Who cares?" Mariah retorted. " I don't like her."

"Right now I don't like *you*, so we're in the same boat."

"Kids, that's enough." Standing, Graham gestured to their vacant chairs with a nod of his head. "Everyone have a seat. Things are getting out of hand."

"But, Dad—"

"Sit, Mariah. You, too, boys."

Jackson knew better than to argue with his dad and returned to his seat. He'd lost his appetite, had zero desire to eat, but he guzzled down his wine as if it was water. He glanced around the room, staring everywhere but at his family. The dining room was just off the kitchen area, a large, but cozy space with ivory walls, stained-glass windows overlooking the sprawling grounds, glittering chandeliers and decorative vases brimming with colored tulips. As beautiful as the room was, Jackson still felt trapped, as if he was in a jail cell, and he was anxious to leave.

"Draysons stick together," Graham said sternly, making eye contact with each one of them. "We don't tear each other down. *Ever*. Regardless of how bad things get."

Smoothing a hand over his mustache, his father gave him a pointed look. Jackson knew what his dad was thinking, knew he held him responsible for the argument with his siblings. Graham had never dated anyone besides Nadia, and had a hard time understanding why Jackson enjoyed playing the field. Though since meeting Grace he hadn't looked at another girl.

"Dad's right. Jack, I'm sorry. I never should have doubted you. Do you forgive me?"

Jackson cracked a sly smile. "I will, Mariah, if you do the early morning shift tomorrow!"

His sister laughed and Jackson chuckled, too, was relieved they were cool again.

"Watching you kids work together, and seeing all that you've accomplished with the bakery has made your father and I extremely proud."

Wide-eyed, Jackson stared at his mother in disbelief. "Really?" he said, unable to hide his surprise. "Three months ago you said I was squandering my life away at Lillian's, and embarrassing you, as well. You said, and I quote, 'Quit baking cakes, and get a real job.'"

"I owe you an apology, son." Nadia wiped at her eyes with the back of her hands. "Actually, I owe all of you an apology. I'm sorry for ever doubting your ability to succeed at Lillian's and for not supporting you. Can you find it in your hearts to forgive me?"

Mariah rubbed Nadia's back. "Of course, Mom. After all, you taught us everything we know about baking."

"I'll be proud to introduce my talented, successful children as master bakers at Sunday's charity gala and I'd also like to hire Lillian's to cater the event. Think you guys can make enough desserts to feed three hundred people?"

"What do you think, Jack? Can we?" Mariah asked with a small smile.

"In light of everything that's happened this week I should probably lay low. Maybe Kelsey or one of the other baristas can help you."

Chase clapped Jackson on the shoulder. "Man, get out of here. If not for you the bakery wouldn't be as popular as it is, and the competition wouldn't be stealing our recipes!"

Jackson hung his head, realizing how foolish he'd been to defend Grace to his family. Someone had stolen the Draynut recipe out of the recipe binder in the kitchen. Grace was the only person who had motive and opportunity. As much as he loved her and wanted to be with her, he had to keep his distance. His family was right; she'd tricked him, but he'd been too blind to see. *First Mimi and now Grace. Do I have the worst track record with women or what?*

"I was wrong. Grace is trouble, so I'm going to keep my distance. Let's pop the bubbly and celebrate. I'm single again!" he said dryly, raising his glass in the air.

"Jack, are you sure that's what you want?" his dad asked, his tone filled with concern. "It's obvious you care deeply about Grace, and it pains me to see you upset."

A bitter taste filled his mouth, coating his tongue, but he was man enough to admit his mistakes and speak the truth. "Chase and Mariah were right. I never should have pursued Grace. She's the enemy—"

"That's not what I said, bro."

"Chase, that's exactly what you said."

"Date her, just keep her out of the kitchen," Mariah said, piping up. "I trust you, Jackson, and if you believe in Grace then I believe in her, too. I'd never do anything to stand in the way of true love, and above all I want you to be happy."

"I don't have a problem with Grace, per se," Chase explained. "It's her father who worries me the most. From what I've heard, Doug Nicholas has no conscience, and will do anything to bury his competitors."

"You're dating Grace Nicholas, too?"

Jackson cranked his head to the right. "Mom, what are you talking about?"

"Meredith Ventura and I have mutual friends, and last week at the country club she went on and on about Grace Nicholas being the perfect woman for her son. Apparently, the two have been seeing each other for several weeks, and Ainsworth is completely smitten with her."

I never saw this coming. Not in a million years. Pain reverberated through Jackson's body. He saw the sympathetic expressions on his parents' faces, watched his siblings share a knowing look and slumped back in his chair. How could he have been so stupid? So blind? Grace had tricked him, and he'd played right into her hands.

"Bro, don't sweat it," Chase said. "You'll have another honey in no time."

To save face, Jackson winked and flashed a broad grin. But he knew in his heart he'd never find a woman as special as Grace.

Chapter 17

"This day is going from bad to worse," Grace grumbled as she spotted Mariah Drayson breeze through the front doors of Samson's Gym on Saturday afternoon. *Oh, brother, what now? What is she doing here? Shouldn't she be at Bite of Seattle?* Looking fit and trendy in her black Puma exercise gear, Mariah whipped off her sunglasses and glanced around the cardio room.

Hoping to avoid detection, Grace ducked behind the magazine stand, pretending to read the glossy tabloid covers. Once a week, Grace did a fitness class with her roller derby teammates, and while doing squats, high kicks and planks they strategized for matches. Her friends were already warming up in Studio A, and Grace didn't have the time or the energy to argue with Jackson's sister. She hadn't had a good night's sleep since Jackson dumped her, couldn't stop replaying their argument in her mind. Thoughts of him dominated her dreams at night, and the more she tried to censure her thoughts, the worse she felt.

Grace released a deep sigh, wondering if the pain in her heart would ever subside. She'd planned to attend Bite of Seattle that weekend, but after overhearing her father's twisted plan on Friday morning—to give away hundreds of Chocolate Explosion desserts to stick it to the Draysons—she'd changed her mind. She wanted nothing to do with hurting the man she loved.

Hoping her nemesis wouldn't find her, Grace bent down behind the water fountain and retied her neon pink sneakers. Approaching with the stealth of a burglar, Mariah sidled up beside her, blocking the sunshine streaming through the windows, but Grace refused to acknowledge her. The music inside the cardio room was deafening, blaring from the overhead speakers, but she heard Mariah's voice loud and clear.

"It's nice to see you again, Grace."

Grace choked on her tongue. *As if!* Mariah despised her, went out of her way to avoid her whenever she used to stop by Lillian's to see Jackson, and Grace thought she was a snob with no manners. Standing, she regarded the petite baker, making no attempt to hide her disdain.

"I was hoping to run into you at the Bite of Seattle this weekend, but you've been missing in action. Is, ah, everything okay?"

What do you *think? Your brother dumped me and he won't return my calls. Of course I'm* not *okay!* Scared her voice would crack if she spoke, Grace put her water bottle to her lips and took a long drink. "What are you doing here?"

Mariah frowned. "Excuse me? I've been coming to this gym for years."

"Then how come I've never seen you here before today?"

"Because my schedule is jam-packed and my amazing fiancé has been keeping me busy in the evenings. You know how it is. You start dating a great guy, then ditch your daily workouts to spend more time with him."

I know all too well, Grace thought sadly. *When I'm with Jackson nothing else matters.*

"I was hoping we could talk."

"I have nothing to say to you."

"Hear me out," Mariah pleaded.

"What do you want? My aerobics class just started and I don't want to miss it."

It was a lie, but Grace had nothing to say to Mariah and wanted her gone.

"We need to clear the air and I figured this was as good a place as any."

"I'm sure you know Jackson dumped me, so cut the nice-girl act, because I'm not buying it." Grace narrowed her gaze. "You're here to gloat, aren't you? Real mature, Mariah."

"That's not why I'm here."

A group of women approached and Grace stepped aside to let the trio pass. She wanted to leave, but something compelled her to stay. "Out with it, Mariah. I don't have all day."

"I won't lie. I've been suspicious of you ever since I caught you making out in the storage room fridge with my brother, but it was wrong of me to judge you because of your last name. I forgive you for stealing the Draynut recipe, but if you hurt Jack again I'll—"

"I didn't steal it!" Grace shouted, throwing her hands up in the air.

Her eyes widened with surprise and curiosity. "You didn't?"

"No. I've never even seen the recipe, nor do I want to."

"And that's the truth?"

"I love your…" Overcome with emotion, Grace trailed off speaking for fear of bursting into tears. "I adore your brother, and I'd never do anything to hurt him. He's special to me, and I only want the best for him."

Happiness covered Mariah's face. "Have you told Jack how you feel?"

"Yes, but he doesn't believe me, and that's okay. I get it."

Her smile faltered. "Get what? I'm confused."

"I'd never betray Jackson, but I'm pretty sure my father had something to do with stealing the recipe," she said sadly. "I'm Doug Nicholas's daughter, and that will never change so I'll stay on my side of the city, and you Draysons stay on yours. Problem solved."

"Not if you're miserable, and I suspect that you are. Just like my brother."

Grace had a million questions for Mariah, was dying to know how Jackson was doing, but she couldn't bring herself to ask. "I have to go."

"The Bite of Seattle ends tomorrow," Mariah said. "Jack's competing in the Bite Cook-Off at eleven o'clock. You should come out and cheer him on."

"Why? So he can insult me again? No, thanks."

"Jack loves you, Grace. I see it in his eyes every time he says your name."

"No, he doesn't." Haunted by the memory of their

breakup, a cold chill whipped through her body and she hugged her hands to her chest. "If he loved me he wouldn't have hurt me."

"Sometimes when people are upset they say things they don't mean."

Grace opened her mouth, realized she didn't have anything to say in response and slammed it shut. She had to admit that Mariah made a good point. Before their argument, Jackson had never yelled at her, let alone raised his voice, and had always been gentle with her. "Does Jackson know you're here? Talking to me right now?"

Mariah shook her head. "No way. He's been a sour-puss all week, so I've been staying *far* away from him. I can't help feeling responsible for his foul mood. My accusations built a wedge between you guys, and I'll do anything to make things right."

Grace believed her. She sounded sincere, and her face was filled with concern.

"I hope to see you tomorrow at Bite of Seattle," Mariah continued. "Come by the Lillian's booth. I'll make you a Draynut, free of charge. It's the least I can do. "

Hearing noises behind her, Grace glanced over her shoulder and smiled at her teammates. They beckoned to her from inside Studio A and she held up a hand, signaling she'd be there in five minutes.

"They look like a rough bunch." Mariah shivered. "Are they wrestlers?"

Grace laughed. "No, but don't mess with me or the Curvy Crashers will get you!"

"That's my cue to leave," she said with a laugh. "Will I see you tomorrow?"

"I don't know. I'll think about it."

"Fair enough. Enjoy your workout."

Grace watched Mariah exit the cardio room. Was she telling the truth? Did Jackson miss her? She shook her head, and the thought from her mind. It didn't matter. He hadn't answered her calls or texts, and after everything he'd put her through in the past week she'd started to think maybe their breakup was for the best. Her cell phone rang and Grace took it out of her pocket. "Hey, Bronwyn, what's up? I thought you were coming to class tonight."

"I changed my mind. Rodolfo wanted to check out the…"

Grace had to plug her left ear to hear what her best friend was saying. "You're where?" she asked, raising her voice to be heard above the noise on the phone line.

"Bite of Seattle. We sampled every booth and now we're so full we can't move. Help!"

"No worries. You guys have fun and I'll talk to you tomorrow—"

"Jackson's here."

"Of course he is," she said, speaking up in spite of the lump in the back of her throat. "He's part owner of Lillian's and a brilliant baker, as well. He *has* to be there."

"If you hurry you can make it down here before the festival ends at nine o'clock."

"I can't." Noting the time, she strode past the free weights towards Studio A. "Booty boot camp 101 is about to start and the girls are waiting for me."

"All right. I understand. I just wanted to give you a heads-up."

"A heads-up about what? What's going on? Is Jackson okay?"

"I'd say! He's surrounded by a bevy of beauties and they're literally eating out of the palm of his hand," Bronwyn reported, her tone thick with disapproval. "If he was my man I'd fly down here and tell the vultures to back off. But that's just me."

Grace forced a laugh to prevent tears from forming in her eyes. It was a lie. Jackson didn't miss her. Didn't want to reunite. If he did, he'd be with her instead of charming the masses at Bite of Seattle. "Girl, we'll talk tomorrow. Have a good night."

Ending the call, she entered Studio A. Her teammates cheered, and Grace rolled her eyes to the ceiling. The instructor, a slender Trinidadian woman with auburn twists, stood in front of the class, shouting instructions to the all-female group.

"Now that we're warmed up, it's time to get down!" the instructor shouted.

Having taken the class before, Grace followed along with ease. She was broken inside, couldn't stop thinking about Jackson with other women, but an odd thing happened as she danced and gyrated to the hip-hop music. Her mood improved, brightening as cherished memories of Jackson flooded her mind. He represented stability, love and family, and Grace wasn't ready to give up on their relationship yet. Tomorrow, she was going to come clean to Jackson about everything—her father's shady business practices, her friendship with Ainsworth, her dreams for their future—and hoped he'd still want her. Grace couldn't wait to see Jackson again, and thanks to his sister she knew exactly where to find him.

Chapter 18

Jackson slammed the driver's-side door, tucked his cell phone into his back pocket and fell into step beside Chase and Mariah. Attending Bite of Seattle, the three-day food festival held on the Seattle Center grounds, had been a Drayson family tradition for years, and as Jackson strolled down the street with his siblings, fond memories from his childhood warmed his heart.

The mood was jovial, the crowd thick, and there were enticing aromas in the air. Magicians did eye-popping tricks, cartoon characters posed for pictures with adoring, pint-sized fans and food vendors offered free samples to attract customers. Foodies of all ages wandered the grounds, desperate to get their hands on some mouth-watering grub—Jackson included. He'd skipped breakfast that morning, but planned to make a pit stop at the Lillian's booth before heading to the main stage. Jackson frowned. *Or maybe not.* The line was a mile long, but seeing customers devour their baked goods filled him with pride.

His gaze landed on a poster, suspended from a tree, and the smile slid off his face. Jackson couldn't go anywhere in the city without seeing signs for Chocolate Explosion, and every time he heard one of Sweetness Bakery's new radio ads he thought about Grace, remembering all of the good times they'd shared.

"We should head to the main stage," Chase said. "It's ten fifteen, and the cook-off starts at—"

"I know what time it starts," he snapped, cutting off his brother midsentence. "You don't have to remind me. I'm not a kid."

Chase stopped walking and stared him down. "You know what? You've been a jerk all week and I'm sick of it."

Riddled with guilt, Jackson hung his head. It wasn't his brother's fault Grace had screwed him over, so why was he taking his frustrations out on him? On everyone? He'd been irritable since breaking up with Grace, and everyone at the bakery was keeping their distance. Jackson didn't blame them. He was on edge, moody, but he didn't know how to pull himself out of his funk. On Thursday he'd coached his basketball team to victory, yesterday he'd gone to a movie with his dad and that morning he'd gone for a jog, but nothing helped. Every day without Grace was torture. Excruciating. What was wrong with him? How could he miss a woman who'd used him for her own selfish gain? Who'd been dating another guy their entire relationship?

"You made it!" Mariah shrieked.

His Chicago cousins, Belinda Drayson-Jones Anthony, Shari Drayson Robinson and Carter Drayson approached, smiling and waving, and the group exchanged hugs and fist bumps. "How is the family?" Jackson asked. "Everything good in Chi-town?"

"Couldn't be better," Shari said brightly. Five feet tall with a round face and ample curves, she looked model-pretty in her coral sundress, gold accessories and sandals. "Business is booming and our latest ad campaign is a roaring success!"

"We heard about the stolen Draynut recipe," Carter said, a scowl creasing his brow. Well-groomed, with short hair and brown eyes, the baker was like chocolate to most women: simply irresistible. Head over heels in love with his wife, Lorraine Hawthorne Hayes, he seemed oblivious to the women on the street staring at him. "Do you have any idea who the culprit is?"

Jackson shook his head, recalling how his great-aunt Lillian had posed the exact same question yesterday afternoon when they'd met at the bakery to discuss the stolen recipe. She'd interviewed the entire staff—including the cleaners and delivery guys—and her tough, hard-hitting questions had shocked everyone. Still, they had no leads.

"Chase, have you noticed an impact on sales since Sweetness debuted their Chocolate Explosion?" Curvy, with brown eyes and long straight hair, Belinda was the kind of woman who attracted male attention wherever she went. Hardworking and goal-oriented, the Chicago baker wasn't happy with herself—or anyone else—unless everything in her life was perfect, and since arriving in Seattle last night she'd made it her mission to uncover the truth.

"It's only been a short time, so it's too soon to tell, but—"

"I'm not worried," Jackson said, bumping elbows with Chase to make amends for snapping at him earlier. "We have the better product, the better staff and the smarter, sexier owners, so the competition doesn't stand a chance!"

Everyone laughed, fervently agreeing that Jackson was right.

"Seeing you together warms the cockles of my heart…"

Jackson raised an eyebrow. *Warmed her what?* His great-aunt Lillian Reynolds-Drayson appeared at his side, looking sophisticated and regal in her pastel pink suit, Chanel scarf and pearl stud earrings. The family matriarch of the Drayson clan was a thin woman with a full head of white hair, but at seventy-nine she showed no signs of slowing down.

"It's always been my fervent hope that each of you would not only succeed in life, but support one another, and I'm thrilled to see your bond growing. Nothing is more important than family. Never forget that."

Belinda and Shari each gave Jackson a one-arm hug and a smile tugged at his lips. His sister was right; his Chicago relatives weren't so bad. Since they'd opened Lillian's of Seattle several months ago, his cousins had been their biggest supporters, and Jackson appreciated their wisdom and guidance. Going forward, he'd make a concerted effort to spend more time with his cousins. They were family, and as Lillian had said earlier, they had to stick together.

"Jack, you're looking fetching this morning," Lillian said, patting his forearm. "It's time you took a bride, and I know just the girl. How do you feel about relocating to Chicago?"

I don't want anyone but Grace, he thought sadly, hating himself for wanting her. *I wish things had been different. I wish she'd loved me as much as I love her.* "I'm too busy at the bakery to date, Aunt Lillian. It's my number-one priority right now."

Her smile was as dazzling as the diamond broach pinned to her blazer. "I understand. I know how demanding work can be, and I'd hate to do anything to curtail the bakery's success."

"It must be something in the genes," Shari said, "Because I'm a workaholic, too, and proud of it!"

Everyone laughed. Jackson mouthed *thank you* to Shari and she winked. Glancing at the booth for Lillian's, which was busier than ever, he made a mental note to speak to Shari about his promotional ideas for the bakery after the cooking competition.

"Girls, how do I look?" Lillian asked, addressing her nieces. "I'd planned to wear a black Diane von Furstenberg sheath dress, but there's a stain on the hem and I didn't want to embarrass myself or the family by wearing something filthy…"

Jackson inhaled the sweet-smelling air, admired the radiant blue sky and reflected on the afternoon Grace had surprised him with a romantic picnic at Discovery Park. They'd fed each other, listened to R&B music on his cell phone, had even danced. The memories of that bright, sunny afternoon caused him to choke up. Would it always be this way? Would he ever get over Grace? Or, would he think about her every single day for the rest of his life?

"Are you ready to charm the Bite of Seattle crowd,

my dear boy?" asked Lillian. "It's time for the Bite Cook-Off, and I'd hate to keep our fans waiting."

Jackson didn't want to go to the main stage, wished he'd never agreed to be a celebrity chef or participate in the Bite Cook-Off with his great-aunt. She was the heart and soul of the business, not him, and he could kick himself for letting Chase and Mariah talk him into doing something he wasn't up to. "As ready as I'll ever be, Aunt Lillian, so let's do this!"

Twenty minutes later, Jackson and Lillian were standing to the left of the main stage. It was equipped with everything they'd need for the competition—utensils, cooking supplies, a microwave and even a state-of-the-art oven.

Jackson could feel the excitement in the air, and made up his mind to give the audience one hell of a show. It wasn't about him; it was about putting his family bakery on the map. Winning the baking competition and being crowned the Bite Cooks Master would definitely increase sales, and since it was the last day of the festival he had to bring his A game.

"Welcome to the Bite Cook-Off!" The female host stood onstage, waving at the audience. People were eating, talking and cheering, and the crowd was so large Jackson couldn't find their family members anywhere.

"Joining me onstage now are Lillian Reynolds-Drayson and Jackson Drayson," the host continued. "Jackson is one of the owners of Lillian's of Seattle, a fantastic new bakery in the Denny Triangle—and an offshoot of the famed Lillian's bakery in Chicago."

Offering his arm, Jackson helped Lillian up the steps and joined the host in the kitchen.

"I tried the Draynut this morning and thought I'd

died and gone to pastry heaven!" she shrieked. "Before we get started, tell the audience how Lillian's of Seattle came about, and some of the challenges you've faced being the new kid on the block, so to speak."

If you only knew! Jackson thought. All week there'd been a lot of buzz around town about Lillian's versus Sweetness, and if the public knew how real the fight was between the bakeries they'd be champing at the bit for all of the salacious details.

"Thank you for having us, Felicity. It's wonderful to be here," Jackson said, with a broad smile. "In the fifties, my great-aunt Lillian was a single mother with a hope and a dream. Working in a Chicago cafeteria, she'd bake special orders for her lunch customers, and when demand grew for her pastries, she quit the cafeteria and rented out a tiny storefront. From these modest beginnings grew a family dynasty."

The crowd cheered and whistled, and Lillian beamed with pride. "I'm thrilled about what my siblings and I have accomplished since the Seattle location opened earlier this year, and I'm excited about..." Jackson spotted a familiar face in the audience and lost his voice. Grace! She was standing at the edge of the crowd, staring at him, love shimmering in her eyes. She looked tired, as though she hadn't slept in weeks, but beautiful nonetheless. Her hair was curled, just the way he liked it, and her loose-flowing multi-colored dress made her look like a bohemian princess. *His* bohemian princess. The woman he loved was in the audience, and he had to speak to her. Now. Couldn't let this opportunity pass him by. Grace was the kind of woman who only came along once in a lifetime, and he didn't want to lose her. That didn't mean Jackson was cool with her dating other guys—he wasn't—but he was confident they could work things out.

"You're excited about…" the host prompted, her voice tinged with anxiety.

Jackson had dreamed about this moment all week, knew exactly what he'd do when he saw Grace again, but shocked himself—and probably everyone in the audience—by doing the unthinkable. He marched across the stage, jogged down the steps and weaved his way through the crowd toward Grace. Running toward him, she threw herself into his open arms.

Relief flooded Jackson's body. No, it was more than relief. It was joy, elation. Grace was back and they were going to work things out. His life *wasn't* over. In fact, it was just beginning.

"Do you have any idea how much I've missed you?" he murmured into her ear, inhaling her fragrant scent. "Baby, I'm sorry. I lost my temper, but I never meant to hurt you."

"I'm sorry, too. I should have told you about my dad, and Ainsworth, and—"

"Are you dating him?" Jackson held his breath. The word on the street was that Grace and Ainsworth were a hot new couple, and he was dying to know if it was true.

"No, Jackson, I'm not. He's a family friend, and nothing more," she said, reaching out and gently caressing his face "You're the only man I want, the only man I love. You have to believe me, baby."

He sighed, relieved the rumor mill had gotten it wrong.

"It was foolish of us to embark on a relationship we knew wouldn't work," Grace said.

Taking her hand, Jackson led her to a quiet corner of the grounds.

"Can I ask you something?"

Jackson nodded. "Of course. Ask me anything. I want everything to be out in the open."

"How could you think that I'd ever betray you?"

He didn't know what to say to her in his defense, couldn't find his voice.

"I thought we had something special, and now I don't know what to think."

"Grace, we *do* have something special."

"No, we don't. If we did you would have believed me when I said I didn't steal the Draynut recipe," she said. "Why didn't you give me the benefit of the doubt? An opportunity to defend myself?"

"Because the last time I gave someone the benefit of the doubt I got screwed."

"What happened?"

Jackson blew out a deep breath. He didn't want to talk about Mimi, but recognized he couldn't move forward with Grace until he opened up to her about his broken engagement and his ex-fiancée's deception. "Three months after Mimi proposed to me I discovered she'd learned my PIN number, and was helping herself to my poker winnings."

Moving closer to him, her face filled with concern, she slowly caressed his shoulders.

"Mimi denied it, of course. Swore on her mother's grave she never touched a dime and I foolishly believed her." He tried to govern his feelings, but his anger broke through and seeped into his tone. "I was embarrassed and wanted to put the incident behind me, but Chase forced me to meet with bank officials. Mimi wasn't on the video footage, but her ex-boyfriend was, so I knew they'd cooked up the scheme together."

"That's horrible, Jackson."

"I never recouped the eighty grand she stole, but that wasn't the worst part. My mom adored Mimi—hell, my entire family did—and she played with their emotions. To this day they think I was the one who messed up, and I don't have the heart to tell them the truth."

Laughter rippled through the crowd as his great-aunt filled in for him. No surprise. His aunt was loved by all, and made friends wherever she went. Having left Lillian in the lurch, Jackson knew he had to return to the stage, but first he had to smooth things over with the woman he loved. "Grace, I believe you. And, you're right, I never should have doubted you for a second. I was angry but deep down I knew you would never steal Lillian's recipes and pass them off as your own. That's not you."

Grace released an audible sigh. "Knowing that you believe me is a huge relief."

"You're my everything, Grace, and I don't want to lose you again."

She fell silent, and Jackson wondered what she was thinking.

"I don't have any proof, but I'm pretty sure my dad had something to do with the stolen Draynut recipe," she said quietly, biting her bottom lip. "I'm disappointed in him, and I hate what he did, but I'm still his daughter and I won't turn my back on him."

"I'm not asking you to."

Her eyes brightened with hope. "You're not?"

"No." Jackson pulled Grace into his arms and kissed her hair. "Baby, nothing is impossible. If we want to be together we'll find a way to make it work."

"The odds are against us."

"I don't care. You're my girl, and I'll move heaven and earth to be with you."

Grace smiled, and Jackson knew he was making progress with her.

"I want you to be my guest at tonight's charity gala. It's being held at the Four Seasons to commemorate the end of Bite of Seattle. All of the money raised will be donated to local charities," he explained. "Please say you'll come. I need you by my side, and I want you to meet my parents and the rest of my family."

She didn't respond, and he feared she was going to turn him down.

"I'll pay for your gown and I'll send a car service to pick you up, as well."

"No, thank you," Grace said, curls tumbling about her pretty face as she shook her head. "I have lots of designer dresses and I can drive myself. I have a Jaguar, you know!"

Jackson chuckled. "I have to get back onstage. I hope to see you later."

Reassured by her smile, he kissed her softly on the lips. Jackson could do anything he put his mind to, and as he jogged back to the stage he decided the charity ball was the perfect venue to prove his love to Grace.

Chapter 19

The glass-and-marble-filled lobby of the Four Seasons Hotel was packed with so many socialites, celebrities and influential businessmen Grace thought she was at a political convention. The luxury downtown hotel was only blocks away from the Space Needle, and the perfect venue for a black-tie event. Hundreds of people, decked out in tuxedos, floor-length gowns and diamonds, were milling about, networking and socializing.

Approaching the ballroom, Grace was shocked to see her dad pacing in front of the double doors. He had a troubled expression on his face and seemed oblivious to the stares he was receiving from silver-haired guests who reeked of old money. Casually dressed in a T-shirt and faded blue jeans, her dad looked out of place among Seattle's elite movers and shakers.

"Dad, what are you doing here?" Grace asked, approaching him. "Is everything okay?"

He stopped pacing, clutched her shoulders and stared deep into her eyes.

"What is it? You're scaring me."

"It was me. I did it."

Dread coated her stomach. "Did what?"

"I planted a college intern at Lillian's to steal the Draynut recipe."

Her heart plunged to her feet. Her dad had confirmed her suspicions, but instead of feeling relieved that he'd finally confessed, Grace felt worse. "Dad, no, how could you?"

"I'm embarrassed about what I did," he said, raking a hand over his hair. "It was foolish of me to think I could succeed by screwing Lillian's over, and I hope you'll find it in your heart to forgive me. I wanted to honor your mother's legacy, but went about it the wrong way."

Unable to speak, Grace swallowed hard.

"Pumpkin, I've thought a lot about your promotional ideas, and I think it's time we implement some of them." Taking her hand in his, he spoke with pride. "Poetry Fridays and Talent Night Saturdays will be a hit. I know it."

"I agree. We're going to knock 'em dead!" Grace smiled, to prove to her dad he had her support, but her heart was full of sadness. What would Jackson do when the truth came out? Would he still love her? Would his family make him choose between them and her?

"I caught a glimpse of you with Jackson Drayson this morning at Bite of Seattle. It's obvious you love him, and seeing you happy and content makes me happy."

Sensing a presence, Grace glanced around the lobby. Jackson appeared at her side and she sucked in a shaky breath. How much had he heard? What did he know? He looked debonair in his crisp black tuxedo, and smelled of sandalwood, her favorite masculine scent. Seeing Jackson decked out in designer threads, Grace was reminded of the Heritage Awards dinner weeks earlier, and smiled at the memory of that romantic, passionate night.

"I'm Jackson Drayson, Mr. Nicholas. It's an honor to finally meet you."

"Grace had nothing to do with stolen recipe. I paid Kelsey Andrews to steal it," he blurted out. "I know it was a rotten thing to do, so I'm canceling the Chocolate Explosion ad campaign and pulling the dessert from our menu."

"It takes a strong man to not only admit his mistakes, but to make amends for it," Jackson said. "I appreciate the gesture, Mr. Nicholas, and I'm sure my family will, too."

"Jackson, what are you going to do about Kelsey?" Grace asked. "I know how much you like her, and she's been a huge help to you the last few months."

"I'm going to fire her, and anyone else who helped her. Loyalty means everything to me, and now I know she can't be trusted."

Troubled, Grace fidgeted with her hands. She hated what her father had done, and wished there was something she could do to make it up to Jackson and his siblings.

"Take good care of my daughter, Jackson."

"I will, sir. You have my word."

Grace hugged her dad and kissed his cheek. "Thanks, Dad. I love you."

"I love you, too, pumpkin. Have fun tonight."

Wearing a sad smile, he strode through the lobby, out of the hotel doors and into the balmy summer night.

Grace had no words. Her father's deception saddened her, and she feared the Draysons would hold his mistakes against her.

"I love your dress."

"What? This old thing?" she joked, striking a pose.

Jackson chuckled and happiness bloomed inside her heart. Wanting to impress him, she'd selected an empire waist gown with crystals along the bodice, and paired it with satin high heels. Admiration shone in his eyes and Grace knew she'd chosen wisely.

"You look like an ebony princess."

"Why, thank you, Mr. Drayson. That's *just* the look I was going for."

"I'm so glad you're here. I was scared you wouldn't come."

"I'm scared, too, Jackson, but I'm willing to break the rules with you."

"How ironic," he said, a pensive expression on his face. "Because seeing you in this stunning white dress makes me want to get all traditional with you."

Her ears tingled. "Wh-what are you saying?"

"What if we eloped, and relocated to New York?"

"Elope?" Grace squeaked. "We can't elope."

"Of course we can. I know it seems sudden, but it feels right. *We* feel right."

His words, and his smile, touched her heart.

"It's not as if I was born to be a baker," he continued. "I've had lots of great careers over the years, and I've never had trouble finding a job. Furthermore, you've always dreamed of moving to the Big Apple, and I want to make your dreams come true."

Mindful of his feelings, Grace chose her words carefully. "I want to marry you, but we can't elope to New

York. It's important to me to have our friends and family there, and I don't want to upset the people we love by shutting them out of the biggest day of our lives."

"I never looked at it that way," he said.

"Furthermore, I don't want to be the reason why you pull out of Lillian's of Seattle." Caressing his face, she tenderly stroked his chiseled features. "Don't you want to see what you could accomplish if you stuck with the bakery for a while?"

"I intend to stick with you forever." Jackson wore an impish smile. Gazing at her, he drew her to him, wrapping his arms possessively around her waist.

"Baby, I can't wait to see what you do with the bakery. You've been successful at the things you've done short-term, so imagine what you could accomplish at the bakery over time. What we could accomplish together if we worked as a team."

"I know one thing I'd like to accomplish with you…"

"Do tell," she cooed, loving their playful banter and the broad, sexy grin on his mouth.

"I'm staying in the penthouse suite, so let's go upstairs and break as many rules as we can think of." He added, "And, this time we won't have to worry about the boys in blue showing up!"

"I'd love to, but *first* I have to meet your parents. I've wanted to meet them for quite some time and this is the perfect opportunity, don't you think?"

"Damn, I wish you weren't so responsible!" Jackson gave her a peck on the lips, then straightened to his full height and offered his forearm. "Ready to meet my family?"

Grace wet her lips with her tongue, wishing her throat wasn't bone-dry. Their arrival at the charity gala was sure to raise a few eyebrows, but she didn't care what anyone thought and snuggled against her man. "I'd love to. Lead the way."

With floor-to-ceiling windows providing spectacular views of Elliott Bay and Puget Sound, the grand ballroom held a magical, enchanted feel. The turquoise water, tall, majestic mountains and pinkish-orange sunset in the background were breathtaking. Professional athletes, TV personalities and celebrity impersonators were on hand signing autographs, and caricature artists sketched images of guests. The five-piece band was performing a Frank Sinatra song, but the atmosphere was as loud and as cheerful as a high school pep rally. Couples kissed and laughed, and animated conversation filled the room.

"Wow, I've never seen this many famous faces in one place before," Grace exclaimed, marveling at all of the big names in attendance. "Your mom must have a lot of connections."

"You've seen one celebrity, you've seen them all."

Incredulous, Grace swatted his forearm. "Oh, stop. The only reason you're not schmoozing with the cast of *Models of Miami* is because the line at their table is out the door."

"Why would I want to hang out with a bunch of catty reality stars when I have you?" Jackson asked, his tone as seductive as his gaze. "You're the total package and I know how lucky I am to have a woman like you in my life. That's why I'll never take you for granted."

It was a struggle to keep a straight face, but she gave him a pointed look and hitched a hand to her hips. "You're trying to get in my panties again, aren't you, Drayson?"

"No." Reaching out, he drew his fingers across her cheek, lovingly and tenderly caressing her skin. "These past few weeks with you have been incredible, the best of my life, and if we never make love again it wouldn't change how I feel about you."

Touched by his words, she wanted to wrap her arms around him and kiss him until she was breathless, but they had an audience, and Grace didn't want to offend his family. The Drayson clan was spread out across two tables and everyone was staring at them. The last thing she wanted to do was upset his loved ones, so she wisely kept her hands at her sides, and off his muscled body.

"Grace, this is my family," Jackson announced, gesturing to the wide-eyed, fashionably dressed group. "Family, this is my girlfriend, Grace Nicholas."

Shaking hands with everyone at the table, Grace admired how suave the men looked, how beautiful the women were and how friendly everyone was, especially Jackson's parents. Energized by their enthusiasm, she clasped Jackson's hand and smiled up at him, deeply grateful they'd been given a second chance at love.

"Grace, it's a pleasure to finally meet you," Nadia said brightly. "My son is completely smitten with you, and it's obvious why."

Graham stepped forward and nodded in greeting. "We've heard a lot of great things about you, and we look forward to getting to know you better."

"Thank you, Mr. and Mrs. Drayson. It's an honor to be here, and I appreciate the warm welcome."

Lillian tapped a gold, dainty spoon against her champagne flute and everyone gathered around her, moving in close to hear what she had to say. "Opening Lillian's of Seattle was the smartest decision I've ever made," she confessed with a proud smile. "Not only has it exceeded my expectations and created a bond across the generations, it helped toward repairing the breach that occurred between Oscar and Henry many moons ago..."

Grace caught Mariah staring at her and giggled when Jackson's sister waved frantically.

"Chase, Mariah and Jackson came together to open the best new bakery on the west coast, and in the process found their soul mates, and I couldn't be happier for them." Raising her flute in the air, her gaze landed on her husband of fifty-five years, Henry Drayson. "A good marriage is like a plum pudding. Only those who make it *really* know what goes into it, so work as a team, and never lose sight of your love."

"To true love!" Henry shouted. "May the fairy tale never end!"

"To true love!" the Drayson clan bellowed in one voice, clinking glasses.

Jackson squeezed Grace's hand and she beamed at him, convinced her heart would burst with love and happiness. Feeling her eyes tear up, she circled her arms around his waist, and rested her head on his chest. His closeness and his dreamy cologne set her body on fire, and Grace couldn't wait to get Jackson upstairs to his suite. He must have read her thoughts because he gestured to the ballroom doors, causing Grace to giggle. "I love you, Jackson."

"And, I love you," he whispered. "You'll never have to question my love, and I'll cherish you every day for the rest of our lives, as long as we both shall live."

Jackson stepped forward, dropped to one knee, and clasped Grace's left hand, sending shock waves through her body. *This can't be happening*, she thought. Her knees were knocking together, threatening to give way. *I* must *be dreaming!*

Gazing up at her with love in his eyes, Jackson slid a pear-shaped diamond ring onto her fourth finger, and squeezed her hand.

Emotion clogged her throat, and the room swam out of focus, spinning around her. It was hard to stay in the moment, but she blocked out everything around them and listened intently to what Jackson had to say.

"The first time we met you gave me attitude, and even dissed my pistachio cupcakes, but I didn't let that stop me from pursuing you. I knew in my heart you were the only one for me."

Remembering their infamous meeting weeks earlier at Lillian's made Grace smile. It felt like they'd known each other for years, rather than a few months. She was more comfortable with Jackson than anyone else she'd ever dated and wanted to spend all of her free time with him. He made her laugh, treated her with respect and showered her with love and affection. It was easy to love him, and she did, with every ounce of her being.

"Grace, I love you, with all that I am, and I always will. You will always be the only woman for me," he declared. "I love your wit, your sense of humor, how smart and sophisticated you are…"

His words touched her deeply, filling her with pride.

"You're everything to me," he said, his tone earnest and sincere. "The spring in my step, the beat of my heart, the sprinkles on my cupcake."

Giggling, she couldn't help but laugh at his joke.

"I knew I wanted to marry you the first time we kissed, and my feelings for you have only gotten stronger since Freezergate."

Grace heard chuckles and whistles behind her, and knew Jackson's family had heard about the night they spent in the bakery storage room.

"I've never loved anyone the way I love you and I want us to create more wonderful memories together. I'll bake for you, cheer you on at your roller derby games and whisk you off to New York to watch your beloved Knicks. Marry me, baby, and I promise you won't regret it."

Grace wanted to shout "yes" from the top of her lungs, but it felt like her lips were glued together. Bursting with excitement, she wrapped her arms around his neck, holding him tight.

"The noise is deafening in here," he said, brushing his nose playfully against hers, his hands affectionately patting her hips. "Was that a 'yes'? Will you marry me?"

Grace noticed, for the first time, that the band had stopped playing and everyone in the room was watching them. Smiling through her tears, she fervently nodded her head, and snuggled against him. "When we're together I feel complete, and there's nothing I'd love more than becoming your lawfully wedded wife. I can't wait to become Mrs. Jackson Drayson!"

"How does a Christmas Day wedding sound?"

"Like heaven on earth," she said, tears spilling down her cheeks.

Grace wished her parents were there to celebrate the joyous occasion, but she sensed her mother's presence in the room, and would call her dad later to share her good news.

"I love you," she whispered. "Thank you for believing in me, and for giving me a second chance. You've made me the happiest woman in Seattle!"

A proud smile covered his face. "I aim to please," he said with a wink.

Pressing her lips to his mouth, Grace kissed her new fiancé slowly, deeply, proving to the world that Jackson Drayson—her one-time rival, and biggest competitor—was indeed the man of her dreams.

* * * * *

Passionate payback

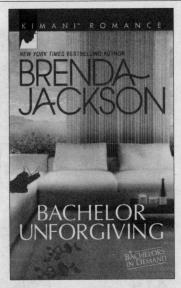

BRENDA JACKSON

BACHELOR UNFORGIVING

Years ago, Kara Goshay believed a vicious lie about Virgil Bougard and ended their relationship. Now his family firm has hired Kara's PR company to revamp his playboy image. But faking a liaison with Kara backfires by a connection so intense it could possibly tame this elusive bachelor at last...

Available July 19!

KPBJ461

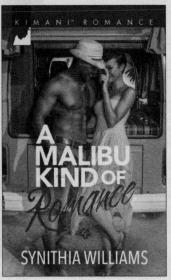

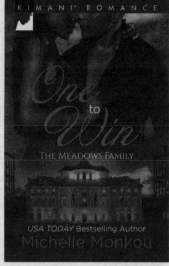

REQUEST YOUR FREE BOOKS!

2 FREE NOVELS
PLUS 2 FREE GIFTS!

KIMANI ™
ROMANCE

Love's ultimate destination!

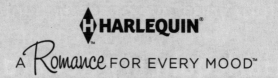

SPECIAL EXCERPT FROM

*In med school, Felicia Blake couldn't help being
impressed by Griffin Kaile's physique, as well as his
intellect. The youngest of the accomplished Blake
triplets, Felicia put aside dating to focus on her
career. She may have fantasized about Griffin, but not
about discovering that he's the biological father of
the baby girl she's been asked to raise. Felicia is the
most stunning woman Griffin has ever known. Now
that the daughter he never knew about has brought
them together, he's eager to explore their romantic
potential. But ambitious Felicia is reluctant to jump
from passion to instant family. Which leaves Griffin
only one choice—to somehow show her that this kind of
breathtaking chemistry occurs only once in a lifetime...*

*Read on for a sneak peek at
TEMPTING THE HEIRESS, the next exciting
installment in author Martha Kennerson's
THE BLAKE SISTERS series!*

"Dr. Griffin Kaile," Felicia said, pulling herself together.
"It's been a while."

"Yes, it has, and you haven't changed a bit. You look
amazing," he said, smiling.

Felicia looked down at her outfit and frowned. "Not
really, but thanks. You look...professional."

Griffin smirked. "Thanks."

Professional. Really, Felicia? "How have you been?" she asked, breaking eye contact when she spied the gift from her sisters—red Valextra Avietta luggage—making its way down the carousel's runway. Felicia reached for the large wheeled trolley.

"I got it," Griffin said, placing his hand over hers.

Griffin's touch sent a charge through her body that she'd only felt one other time before, delivered by the same man. Felicia quickly pulled her hand from his and took a step back. "I'm doing well." Griffin picked up the large bag and placed it next to Felicia before reaching for his own leather suitcase.

"What a gentleman," Felicia heard a woman say.

"Thanks," Felicia said, smiling up at him.

"Last I heard, you were working somewhere overseas," Griffin said.

Felicia nodded. "I've spent the past year working in Asia."

"Wow, I bet that was an adventure. Are you in town long? We should get together…catch up," Griffin suggested, the corner of his mouth rising slowly.

"I…I'd really like that, but I'm only in town for the day. Unexpected and urgent business I have to tend to."

"I can't convince you to extend your trip?" Griffin asked, offering her a wide smile.

Don't miss TEMPTING THE HEIRESS
by Martha Kennerson, available September 2016
wherever Harlequin® Kimani Romance™
books and ebooks are sold!